MW01100584

Danger at Outlaw Creek

~*~
Learn to Read... Read to Learn!
RCSD Highlands Elementary School
& Preschool Library
~*~

Danger at Outlaw Creek

JERRY JERMAN

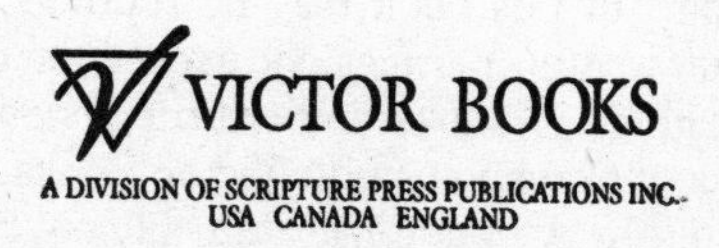

A DIVISION OF SCRIPTURE PRESS PUBLICATIONS INC.
USA CANADA ENGLAND

THE JOURNEYS OF JESSIE LAND

The Long Way Home
My Father the Horse Thief
Phantom of the Pueblo
Danger at Outlaw Creek

Cover design by Scott Rattray
Cover illustration by Michael Garland
Copyediting by Afton Rorvik, Liz Duckworth

This is a work of fiction. Any resemblance to actual events or persons, living or dead, is entirely coincidental.

Library of Congress Cataloging-in-Publication Data

Jerman, Jerry, 1949–
Danger at Outlaw Creek / by Jerry Jerman.
p. cm.—(The Journeys of Jessie Land)
Summary: When twelve-year-old Jessie rejoins her old friend for the filming of a movie in Arizona during the Depression, she encounters dangerous adventures.
ISBN: 1-56476-465-6
[1. Motion pictures—Fiction. 2. Actors and actresses—Fiction. 3. Depressions—1929—Fiction. 4. Adventure and adventurers—Fiction. 5. Arizona—Fiction.] I. Title. II. Series: Jerman, Jerry, 1949– Journeys of Jessie Land.
PZ7.J54Dan 1995
[Fic]—dc20 95-2812
CIP
AC

---

1 2 3 4 5 6 7 8 9 10 Printing/Year 99 98 97 96 95

© 1995 by Jerry Jerman. All rights reserved.
Printed in the United States of America.
No part of this book may be reproduced without written permission, except for brief quotations in books and critical reviews.
For information write Victor Books,
1825 College Avenue, Wheaton, Illinois 60187.

To Laddie and Virginia Herout

Chapter 1

The train chugged noisily into the station. Looking past my reflection in the window, I saw no trace of Tom. Where on earth was he? On a splintered sign I read the name of the town—Flintrock, Ariz.—painted in black, dripping letters. Beside it I spied a faded, yellow train station, the stucco crumbling at the corners. A woman and child sat on a sun-blistered bench with bags at their feet. The woman held up a newspaper with a large headline, and I could make out the words ROOSEVELT APPROVES. News about the president. Then steam and dust rose up until all I saw was me.

In the window glass I gazed at my short, red hair, deep brown eyes, determined chin, my clean but frayed white shirt, and my patched overalls. Leaning forward in the itchy train seat, I thought, *Jessie Land, what possible help could you be to Tom in this forlorn-looking place?*

I unfolded the telegram I'd received from him yesterday. Even now the words seemed to shout with urgency.

> JESSIE COME AT ONCE TO FLINT-
> ROCK ARIZONA STOP YOUR HELP
> SORELY NEEDED STOP TOM

And speaking of Tom McCauley, where on earth was he?

I looked hard but saw no one waiting to greet me that hot June morning in 1935. Fretting Tom's whereabouts, I folded up the telegram. Then I stood in the aisle with my borrowed cardboard suitcase and made my way to the door.

Before I got there, though, Tom appeared at the end of the aisle. He smiled broadly.

"Missy!" he called out, using his nickname for me.

"Tom!" I cried. I ran to my friend, bumping my suitcase along the row of seats. I threw my arms around him and gave him a fierce hug. "I was worried when I didn't see you waiting on the platform."

"I hope you didn't doubt I'd turn up," he said.

When I let loose, Tom held me back some and gave me the once over. I looked up at him. Though no relation to me, Tom I regarded as kin and a joy for my eyes to behold. He stood over six feet tall. His wide-brimmed black hat shaded his kindly face, no longer pale as I had remembered, but now sun-reddened. His blue-veined, wrinkled hand came up and stroked his white moustache. A splash of white beard clung to his chin. He wore a faded purple shirt and black trousers stuffed into a pair of brightly polished green boots. Except for the sunburn, he looked the same as the last time I'd seen him, a few weeks back—when he'd helped me cross half the country to find Mama and Daddy in California.

"You're truly a sight for sore eyes," he told me with a

grin that wrinkled his face.

"What's this all about?" I asked.

Grabbing my suitcase, he simply said, "We'd best hurry. We can talk in the car."

He steered me off the train and onto the wooden station platform. But the moment I stepped out into the bright morning sunlight, I nearly swooned. The heat burned into me something fierce. I'd been around plenty of ovens in my life but never in one. *Goodness!*

"Gotta get used to this climate," Tom advised. "It gets powerful hot early and stays that way till sundown."

He led me to a long, shiny, cream-colored car with silver pipes coming out from under the hood. On the door I saw an oval sign with an old sailing ship on it. Below the blue waves of sea the words ODYSSEY PICTURES were painted in fancy script.

Tom shoved my suitcase behind the front seat and then held open the car door. "Hop in, missy. The studio's got itself a little movie camp just up the road a piece."

I climbed in. Tom shut the door behind me. Already I knew some things about moving pictures, owing to the fact that Daddy worked for the famed Will Rogers on his Santa Monica ranch. Mr. Rogers was the most famous moving picture actor in the world.

But I didn't know much about this moving picture. Or why Tom had sent that telegram to me in Flagstaff where I'd been staying. I just knew that outside Flintrock a moving picture was being made called *Danger at Outlaw Creek.* I also knew that Tom had a job with the moving picture company. Now I guessed he had a job for me.

Tom climbed into the car, yanked off his hat, and threw it into the wide seat between us. He started the engine, and we set out down the hot, dusty street of this southern Arizona town.

"I thought you'd bring your friend Leo along," Tom said, keeping his eyes straight ahead. He was speaking of my almost-brother Leo Little Wolf, an orphan who now lived with me and Mama and Daddy.

"No, he wanted to stay behind in Flagstaff a while," I replied. We'd been visiting a friend, Hazel Womack, when Tom had tracked me down. "I expect Leo'll be along in a couple of days, though."

Tom glanced at me, then frowned at the instrument panel and shook his head. "Yep. Well, I surely hope this picture gets wrapped up in a couple of days. I surely do." His voice and frown told me there must be some kind of trouble.

We rumbled down Flintrock's main street, which had been bricked in places but mostly gave way to dirt. I saw a few folks, women and children mostly, moving slowly down the sidewalk like the heat was a heavy burden they couldn't shrug off. In front of a drugstore at least a dozen men sat on benches or stood around looking tired and unclean. We passed an old hotel, the white stucco peeling to reveal a green layer beneath. Across the street I saw a row of buildings, including a moving picture theater, all boarded up. On one building some words had been scrawled: *Welcome to Flintrock, the town Roosevelt forgot.*

More news of the president, this time bad.

"I got you a room at the hotel, right next to mine," Tom said, pointing back with his thumb. "Most of the movie folks're staying there. We'll check you in later. Maybe after this movie's finished, I'll take you a few miles up north to visit an old ghost town. We shot some scenes out there a couple days ago."

"That'd be exciting," I replied, taking my eyes off the cheerless town and resettling them on Tom. "But what about the moving picture? What's this job you have for me?"

Tom didn't answer. He ran his withered fingers along the dashboard. There was nary a speck of dust on it. "How do you like this vehicle, Jessie? Not much like that old Ford pickup we came west in, is it?"

It didn't take a genius to figure out that Tom was stalling me.

"You didn't send me that telegram for nothing. So you might as well just be out with it."

He grinned, then shoved his hand through his gray hair. "You always get straight to the point, don't you, missy?"

He turned right and we left Flintrock behind us. I spotted dark specks far ahead in the dry, dusty landscape. This country put me in mind of what I'd left behind weeks ago in Liberal, Kansas—the Dust Bowl, the newspapers called it. The only difference here was the craggy rock and mountains in the distance.

"Fact is," Tom said, drawing me back to him, "this

movie's turned into one big mess. And the whole bunch of us'll be out of work if we don't solve our problem."

"What problem?" I asked, plumb out of patience.

"It's our leading lady. Maybe you've heard of her. Name's Winnie Collins."

I stared back at him. "Did I hear you right? I thought I just heard you say 'Winnie Collins.' "

"I did."

I gasped. I laughed out loud. I bounced up and down in the seat, delighted.

"I take it the name's familiar to you," he said.

"Winnie Collins the child moving picture star?" I asked, still not believing my good fortune.

"The very one, though she's not exactly a child no more. She's thirteen, a year older than you."

Excitement bubbled up inside me. I'd seen some of her moving pictures, back in Liberal and in Oklahoma. In my mind I pictured the cute blonde with curly locks and bright blue eyes who sang and danced so well. But something about that image didn't fit well out here.

I said, "I didn't know Winnie Collins made Westerns."

"Well, she don't," Tom sighed, gazing ahead. "Leastwise she don't seem to want to make *this* particular one."

The dark shapes ahead became more distinct. I made out a dozen or more cars and trucks, a line of trailers, boxes of all kinds, and people—far more people than I'd seen back in town. On the outskirts of the camp I glimpsed at least a dozen dirty children slouching about, all seemingly attentive to the activity in the camp.

"Fact is, Winnie's been downright cantankerous," Tom continued. "Way I see it, she's just plain lonely and unhappy. So I figured if she had someone her own age about, she might be more agreeable. And Mr. Dixon, he gave the OK to my sendin' for you. He's willin' to try anything to get this picture finished up."

"Who's Mr. Dixon?" I asked.

"Walt Dixon—the producer and director," Tom explained. "The man in charge of the whole shebang."

"So you want me to keep Winnie Collins company?" I said, excited at the thought.

"That's it," Tom said, braking the vehicle at the edge of the huge settlement of tents and trailers, trucks and automobiles. A cloud of dust foamed up in front of us. The haze made everything look fuzzy and dreamlike. Through the dust I caught glimpses of cowboys and villains with bandannas pulled up over their noses. I saw horses and dance hall ladies in fancy, colorful costumes. These folks looked like they'd been plucked up in 1875 and plopped right smack down in 1935.

" 'Nother thing, missy," Tom said. I turned to him. He wore the kind of frown I'd seen on him when we set out in the car—the expression that told me something was wrong. "This movie business's a strange fandango. Nothin's quite what it seems. And these movie folks don't go 'bout things quite the way me and you would. They tend to fret over the dadburnedest things."

I didn't understand and wanted to ask him more. More about Winnie. More about these moving picture folks. But he climbed out of the car and stalked off into the middle of the hubbub.

"Hey, Tom, wait up!" I yelled.

I yanked open my door and chased after him, taking two steps for every one of his. I paced through the dusty camp, dodging folks every step of the way. I nearly ran right into a lady wearing a red, ruffled dress with white petticoats showing and enough powder on her face for five ladies. I edged around her and nearly caught up with Tom when along came two men carting an Indian totem pole between them. I ducked under the pole and dashed to where Tom had come to a halt.

Looking around him, I spied a mess of lights on long poles and three big, black, boxy things I took to be moving picture cameras. Men in sweat-streaked shirts and hats stood behind the cameras. Beyond them stretched an Old West street scene. A dry goods store, a sheriff's office, a feed store, and a blacksmith's shop lined the dusty street. Then between the storefronts and the cameras I spotted her—Winnie Collins!

She stood in the street with her hands on her hips. Her blond curls bounced as she talked to a short, plump man. She wore a tan cowgirl outfit with a vest and a short skirt with fringe. Her white shirt looked fancy with its puffy sleeves. In the sun her polished boots gleamed. She looked a whole lot older in real life than she did in her moving pictures. Every once in a while she raised her hand and shook the sheaf of papers she held.

Tom stepped closer, so I followed. He said, "Mr. Dixon,

I brought—"

But the short man in front of Winnie waved his hand without even looking back, as if he didn't want to be disturbed. I took it as pure rudeness, but Tom hung back before he finally edged closer. I trailed him, hoping I could hear what went on.

"Look, Winnie, it's going to be a long, hot day," the plump man pleaded. "We need to get this scene wrapped."

Suddenly Winnie Collins threw the pages she held to the ground and stepped on them, mashing them into the dirt with the heel of her shiny boot. One of the pages went flying as the hot breeze caught it and carried it off.

"I cannot work with this *horrid* script!" Winnie cried. "And I hate this *horrid* place!"

"Winnie, listen to reason, please," the man begged.

At once the child star stomped past the short, plump man and came up to Tom and me. "Everyone here is absolutely horrid, horrid, horrid!"

Then pointing a stubby finger at me, she yelled, *"And you're horrid too, whoever you are!"*

Chapter 2

Winnie stalked off into the crowd. Her words stung me. I'd never had a perfect stranger call me "horrid" before.

I turned to tell Tom what I thought of Winnie Collins, but he had bent down to gather up the loose pages that flipped in the breeze.

The director, Mr. Dixon, stood erect, hands on his hips, sturdy as a rock. A short rock. Tom handed the papers to him and stepped back, like a dog fearful of getting kicked.

Then Mr. Dixon turned to me. His dark eyes blinked behind spectacles with black circle frames. His moustache stuck out under his nose like a little gray brush, and his puffy red face looked like it might explode. For some reason he wore a starched khaki outfit, complete with a hard hat, shorts, green knee socks, and brown chunky shoes, like someone on an African safari. His appearance made me want to giggle, but his expression told me to keep still.

Abruptly, he yanked off his hat and hurled it to the ground. On top of his bald head two dark hairs stuck straight up like ant feelers.

"If *that* don't beat all!" the director shouted. He yanked out a gold pocket watch, flipped it open, and scowled.

Then his hand came up and slapped the top of his head, mashing the two lone hairs. "Just look at the *time!* This is a fine pickle. How'd I ever let Iola talk me into shooting in this god-forsaken location? We should've done the whole thing on a sound stage!" He kept slapping the top of his head.

I had to admit these moving picture folks were downright odd.

Tom took my arm and we stepped closer. "Mr. Dixon, this here's Jessie Land," he said.

I nodded at the director, not sure I cared to be introduced at that particular moment. Then Tom fetched the man's hat from the ground, dusted it off, and handed it to him.

Mr. Dixon gave me a skeptical look. "This is your miracle worker?" he asked, blinking at me.

"That's right," Tom answered. "Jessie and her folks live in Santa Monica and—"

"Spare me the biography," he snapped. "She hardly looks like the proper companion for Winnie."

Tom stiffened. "She can do the job awright, Mr. Dixon. I can personally vouch for her."

The director didn't seem convinced of my merits. Probably my worn overalls and chopped-off hair didn't make for a proper impression. I didn't much care. Nor did I care for Mr. Dixon, Winnie Collins, or this whole moving picture set for that matter. I also didn't care for the way Tom acted around these folks—like he was walking on eggs or something.

Still, I felt I should defend myself. "I'm fully capable of taking on any job you might have," I piped up.

Mr. Dixon's bushy eyebrows shot up. "Oh, are you now?"

"Just tell me what you want me to do," I said.

"Get Winnie back on the set. That's what I want you to do," he growled. "We can't afford to lose another minute." He looked hard at Tom. "This idea of yours better work. If it doesn't, we're finished on this picture—and that goes for you too."

He stomped away.

"Just what's going on around here?" I asked Tom.

He grinned at me, but trouble still showed in his eyes. "This picture is way over budget and two weeks behind schedule. Tomorrow morning we've gotta shoot a big, expensive train scene Mr. Dixon's frettin' about. And now Winnie keeps walkin' off the set."

"How'd you ever get hooked up with these unpleasant folks?" I asked.

"These days you take the job that comes along if you want to eat regular," he said. "I feel lucky to have met up with Mr. Dixon when I did. He needed someone on the set to give advice about the Old West."

I knew Tom spoke the truth. A seventy-four-year-old ex-convict would find it hard to get work in 1935. But I knew luck had nothing to do with it. The good Lord had been looking after Tom since I'd seen him last.

Eager to help my friend, I said, "Well, what should I do?"

"Just talk to the girl, missy," he said. "Like a friend, you know? Try to get her to come back and finish her scenes."

"I'll do what I can," I promised.

Tom's smile could not hide the concern in his face. A look he'd worn since he met me at the train.

"Are you all right, Tom?"

He looked about. "Something funny's going on 'round here," he said softly. "I have some suspicions and I aim to talk to Mr. Dixon directly. Tonight maybe."

"What suspicions?"

He ignored my question. Instead, he motioned toward the edge of the camp. "Winnie's dressing room's in a trailer over thataway. It's the—"

"Tom! Tom, over here on the double!" Mr. Dixon's voice boomed.

Tom touched the brim of his black hat and said, "Go on, missy. See what you can do." He took off before I could ask any more questions.

My land, as Mama would've said. I felt plopped down in the middle of a world I couldn't make sense of. I didn't care for it one whit. But I owed Tom more than I could ever repay. I owed him my very life. I owed him my reunion with Mama and Daddy. I knew Tom needed this job, and I promised myself I'd do whatever I could to help him keep it.

So I started working my way back through stacks of boxes and moving picture equipment toward the trailers. There I hoped to find Winnie Collins, though I doubted the child star would put much stock in anything I said to her.

I dodged folks dressed up like cowboys and pioneers and outlaws, and I leaped out of the way of a group of men wearing sweat-soaked undershirts and sunglasses who strained as they carried a large wooden crate.

Near the trailers, I came upon the ragged children I'd seen earlier. I took them to be town kids trying to spy famous folk. They stood in the fierce sun staring at the moving picture crew and equipment like they were the most interesting things to ever hit Flintrock, Arizona. And when I got close, they stared at me.

As I passed, they all stood up, their eyes wide. There looked to be twenty of them, mostly boys.

One of the smaller ones said, "Gee, lookit. It's Winnie Collins!"

An older kid with a smudged, freckled face and a floppy cloth cap punched the smaller one lightly on the arm. "That ain't Winnie Collins, you goose." Then to me he said, "Who're you, miss, if you don't mind my askin'?"

I stepped over to him. He was about my height and my age most likely. His dirty brown hair looked like he'd cut it himself without the benefit of a mirror or reputable scissors.

"Jessie Land," I said, my hand out. "Who're you?"

He gripped my hand but didn't shake it. "Cap McCall. You in this here movie with Winnie Collins?"

"Me?" I said, surprised. "No, I'm just visiting a friend." It was pleasant talking to regular folks again, so I asked,

"What do people do around here?"

"Not much," he shrugged, letting go of my hand. He glanced at the dirt and dug his bare toe in it. "Most folks 'round here are outta work."

"Whatcha talkin' 'bout, Cap," chimed in a tall, thin, red-haired boy. "Least your pa's got hisself a job at the garage." To me he said, "My folks is savin' up to take us to California." The boy's chest swelled out with pride.

I glanced at the redhead's worn gray shirt and thread-bare trousers. Like the rest of them, he wore no shoes. I noticed that three of the boys didn't even wear shirts. One boy had on a pair of pants stitched from a flour sack and a small tin cooking pot perched on his head.

"Folks're out of work in California too," I pointed out to the redhead. "You might be better off staying put."

"Staying *here?*" he whined. "You gotta be kiddin'. Least there's orange groves and canneries out there."

"Yes, and Hoovervilles and migrant camps too."

"Hoovervilles?"

"They're crowded, dirty camps where folks who don't have jobs live," I explained.

"So what's *your* old man do out there? I'll bet he's got hisself a job," he smirked.

"He does," I admitted. "He works for Will Rogers, on his ranch in Santa Monica."

The redhead's eyes opened wide. So did his mouth. I saw he was missing a couple of teeth. "Go on!" he sang out.

"It's true," I said.

"So the truth is you don't want no other folks comin' out there," he told me.

The boy named Cap reached out and grabbed the redhead's arm. "Hey, lay off, Red. She didn't say—"

Red jerked away. "You two belong together," he jeered. "You both think you're better'n the rest of us."

I protested, "I'm just trying to tell you—"

"I *know* what you're trying to tell me," the boy argued. "I've seen the likes of you before. You want to keep all the good things to yourself. Heck, you're probably *lyin'* 'bout your old man workin' for Will Rogers." He turned to the others. "Hey, guys, she's lyin' to us, ain't she?"

"I am not lying!" I cried. I turned and started walking away from him, my hands balled into fists.

"Go on, Miss Fancy Pants!" the red-headed boy hollered after me. "Stay away from us. You might *catch* somethin'!"

The kids laughed, and I hurried toward the trailers. I was angry and confused. Had I been wrong to tell them about the Hoovervilles? Wrong to tell the truth?

No, I thought, *not wrong.* But maybe these kids did need to believe life couldn't be as hard everywhere as it was in Flintrock, Arizona.

Chapter 3

As I walked along the row of trailers, I wished I'd never set foot on this moving picture set. Never stopped to talk to those town kids. Never even met up with the famous Winnie Collins.

My thoughts carried me home as I stopped and stared at the silver trailers, all eight of them gleaming in the fierce sun. If only I were home in Santa Monica with Mama and Daddy, not stuck here among these hostile folks in this hostile heat. I doubted Winnie would come to her senses. Doubted I could do much of anything to get her to cooperate with Mr. Dixon. Maybe I should just tell Tom I didn't want this job and go home.

No, Jessie, I told myself, *you've never been a quitter and this's no time to start.* I had to at least try. After all, Tom was depending on me.

I stopped in front of a trailer with the door cracked open. I heard music coming from inside. Did this one belong to Winnie? I eased up the two steps and tried peeking through the narrow opening.

It was too dark to see in. I tapped lightly on the door and it swung open a little.

Over the music a man's deep voice burst out of the

darkness: "Iola sugar, what're we gonna do now?"

"We're not going to do anything, B.J.," replied a woman with a soft, velvety-smooth voice. "And stop calling me 'sugar'!"

Uh-oh. Wrong trailer. I took a step back and reached out to pull the door closed after me.

"But that old man, McCauley, he *saw* you," the man said. "He knows what you've been up to and he'll go to Dixon."

The mention of Tom's name froze me to the spot. In spite of the heat, a chill swept through me. Tom *had* said he intended to talk to Mr. Dixon about something. Some trouble. Instead of hightailing it out of there like any right-thinking person would have, I leaned closer.

"You leave Walt Dixon to me," the woman replied. "The old man we'll take care of soon. Maybe tonight."

My mouth dropped open. What did she mean "take care of"? I stood for a moment at that door, fretting over what to do next.

Then I knew! I had to tell Tom what I'd heard—and fast! I turned, hopped down the two steps, and ran smack into a man.

He grumbled, "Lookout, kid!" My eyes fixed on the bushel basket he carried in his arms.

Snakes! The basket overflowed with snakes! Dozens of brown, black, and copper heads wiggled toward me. Forked tongues stuck out from their hideous mouths and their flat black eyes stared at me. I leaped back and landed on my rear on the top step of the trailer. The snake-man reached out a hand to help me to my feet, bringing the snakes right up into my face again.

Yikes!

I plowed backward, smashing through the partly opened door.

"Whoa!" I cried out as I tumbled back in the dark room. I hit the floor with a sudden jolt.

I stared wide-eyed at the dark ceiling. A thought hit me. *Snakes! They were just moving picture snakes. Rubber snakes, you fool girl.*

Sighing with relief, I turned and spied a desk with a lamp on it. Beside the desk stood a man and a woman. Looking at me. The scent of the woman's perfume filled the trailer. The music came from a radio on a small table.

I cleared my throat. "Sorry, but this man, he had these . . . snakes," I said, trying to explain.

"Snakes!" shrieked the large man. "Where?"

"Shut up, B.J." the woman said.

In the dim light I saw the woman wore a white dress and had a long, furry thing draped around her neck. Her eyes narrowed at me. Then she bent over the desk and swept something into a canvas bag. As she hurried, I saw a small object fall to the floor.

Gathering up the bag, the woman demanded, "What're you doing in here?"

I sat up, wet my lips, and began, "Well, I was looking for—"

"You've no right to barge in like this," she declared.

I climbed to my feet and tried to explain as I edged

around a box heaped with clothes and backed toward the door.

"Well, you see, I was just . . . Mr. Dixon's the one who—"

"This is a *private* place!" the woman cried. "Do you make it your habit to come barging through closed doors?"

"Sorry, ma'am," I replied, "but, fact is, the door was open."

The woman spun toward the man. He stood much taller than her and seemed as broad as the desk. He wore a tight-fitting brown suit and a derby clearly too small for his head.

"You idiot!" she yelled at him. "Must you always leave doors open?"

The large man scratched his head, knocking his hat to the floor. He mumbled something as he stooped to fetch it.

"What's that?" the woman demanded. "Out with it!" She seemed to have forgotten all about me.

"Gee, Iola sugar, I didn't think nobody would come crashing in on us like that. That girl said something about snakes. I wanna know what she's talking about."

The woman dropped the canvas bag on the desk and crossed the room toward me. "Who are you, dear?" she asked, a phony warmth in her voice.

"Jessie Land," I told her. "I come from Santa Monica, California."

The woman, Iola, hovered near me, the smell of her

perfume making me gag. With the light streaming in from the open door, I got my first good look at her. Her deep green eyes fixed on me as she stroked her pointed chin with long, thin fingers. Her fingernails were blood red. Her short, slicked-down black hair looked like a tight-fitting cap.

"Just what do you think you're doing, dear?" she asked, staring at me.

The thing draped around her neck was the carcass of a white, furry creature. Its dark, blank eyes made me shiver. I wondered what possessed the woman to wear such a thing in this heat. As she stroked the dead critter, she leveled a hard gaze at me. "Well?"

"Iola, don't you think we oughta ask her about them snakes?" the man asked. He had come up behind the woman and kept glancing about the floor as if looking for escaped reptiles.

These two struck me as odd, even by moving picture people standards. I wanted to get far away from them.

Backing into the opened doorway, I said, "Mr. Dixon sent me . . . to talk to Winnie Collins."

"Obviously, dear, Winnie isn't here. Her trailer is on the end."

I nodded at the woman and smiled. "Much obliged." I ducked out the door and raced off.

"Wait!" the woman yelled after me.

But I didn't wait. I scrambled across the hard, dusty ground, putting as much distance as I could between me and that strange pair.

Chapter 4

When I stopped, I found myself right in front of the last trailer. A small cardboard sign stuck on the door read:

MISS WINNIE COLLINS

I knew I had to find Tom and tell him what I'd overheard, but the sign reminded me of the job Tom had given me. Maybe I should talk to Winnie first. After all, Tom's livelihood depended on what she did next. I'd warn him of the plot against him as soon as I talked to Winnie.

As I stepped up to the silver trailer door, I felt uneasy. I glanced down at my patched clothes and my worn shoes. Mr. Dixon had been right. I sure didn't look like a proper companion for a moving picture star. But there was that promise I'd made to help Tom. . . .

I'd do it, foolish as I might appear. I smoothed my hair then rapped my knuckles on the door's hot surface.

"Winnie, it's Jessie Land," I called out, trying to sound pleasant. "Open the door please. I'd like to talk to you."

No answer. I gathered my courage and rapped again. "Winnie? Are you in there?"

All at once the child star's sassy voice burst out. "I

don't know you. *Go away!"*

Star or no star, the girl didn't have a civil bone in her body. I'd have to try a something different, something that might work on a spoiled child actress.

"Please, Winnie," I pleaded. Taking a deep breath, I added, "I've seen all your moving pictures. You're my most favorite star. Won't you please let me in?"

Actually, I'd only seen a few of her moving pictures. And as for her being my favorite star, well, I'd be praying later for forgiveness for that fib too. But my flattery worked. The trailer door cracked open, revealing a narrow slice of Winnie's face.

"You look like one of those ragamuffins from town," she said, indignantly. Then her tone changed abruptly. "So which one is your favorite?"

I let her insult go by. "Favorite what?" I asked.

"Favorite *movie,* you nitwit!" she barked.

At first my mind went blank. Then the image of Winnie surrounded by British soldiers in India popped into my head.

"Why, *The Eastern Star,* of course."

Suddenly the door swung wide. Winnie stepped in front of me. She wore a long, red silken robe and had a yellow towel wrapped around her hair like a turban. Dressed that way with her proud look put me in mind of a princess from the Far East.

"Really?" she said without smiling. *"The Eastern Star?"*

I looked at her and nodded. It wasn't much of a lie, I

reasoned, since it was the only Winnie Collins picture I could think of at the moment.

"I *loved* playing Melissa, and I did a *superb* job of it," she mused, her blue eyes going dreamy for an instant. "The critics just *raved* about me in that part." Then she looked at me directly and declared, "Nothing like this horrid Western."

As she adjusted the towel on her head, I crept past her into the trailer.

"Hey! Wait just a minute, you! I didn't invite you in."

Her cowgirl costume lay heaped in the middle of the floor. On top of the pile I spied Winnie's curly blond locks. A wig! Tom's words came back to me. "Nothin's quite what it seems."

A small, black fan blew the warm air around, not doing much to cool the inside of the stuffy trailer. A pretty, dark green carpet covered the floor. Against one wall sat a beige couch littered with unopened envelopes. Fan mail, I guessed. On a polished wooden table I noticed the biggest radio I'd ever seen and enough food to feed all the hungry kids of Flintrock—a basket of bananas and oranges, half a cake with thick white icing, two opened bottles of cream soda, a few partly eaten cookies, a glass half full of a chocolate malt, and a plate with the remains of mashed potatoes and gravy.

On the walls I saw pictures of Winnie, all decked out with her fake golden locks, fake smile, and a lacy hair bow. I spotted a picture of her with President Roosevelt and another with Will Rogers, my true favorite moving picture star.

From beside the door, the actress declared, "I didn't invite you in here, ragamuffin. What do you want?"

I forced myself to be civil. "Mr. Dixon sent me to talk to you—you know, like friends. He really needs you to finish that scene."

Pouting, she stalked across the room and collapsed on the beige couch. Some of the letters spilled to the floor. "Well, I don't have any friends. And I certainly don't want to finish that scene. It's the *stupidest* scene in this whole stupid movie. Who'd ever believe *I* would be kidnapped by outlaws?"

She had me there. I couldn't imagine a soul ever wanting to kidnap her.

Winnie reached out and plucked up the chocolate malt from the table. She sucked through the straw and finished it off, then kept sucking air. The loud slurping made me want to yank that glass right out of her hand.

I thought for a moment. What could I say to this spoiled, rude girl to convince her to go back to the set? Not a single idea came to me. Finally, I just told her plain, "Mr. Dixon says if you don't go back, it'll ruin the moving picture. And everyone'll be out of work. Surely you don't want to put folks in a fix, do you?"

She looked at me like I was a bug she'd sooner squash.

"What do *I* care?" the actress said. "It's not *my* problem. Besides, I'm sick of this horrid movie. Sick of this horrid place. You have absolutely no idea what *I* have to put up with."

"Well, you're right," I admitted. "I don't know much about the moving picture business. But it seems to me you should appreciate the job you have. Lots of people are out of work these days—like the folks in Flintrock."

"And that's another thing," she complained. "Those filthy children from town who sit around all day staring at me. It's . . . it's *creepy.*"

I remembered the shame of being poor and the ache of going hungry. Her unfeeling words stung. "That's about the most selfish thing I've ever heard anyone say," I snapped.

Winnie's eyes grew large. She slammed the empty glass down, making some cookies bounce off the table.

"You're just one of them!" she shouted. "Nothing but common trash!"

I stiffened, burning with anger. "I'll choose any of them over the likes of you," I fired back.

Her eyes narrowed. As she jabbed a pudgy finger in the direction of the door, the yellow towel fell off, revealing short, mousy brown hair plastered flat against her head.

"Out!" she yelled. "Get out of here, you—you—!"

That suited me just fine. But as I started to leave, Winnie sprang from the couch and grabbed my arm.

"You're worse than a ragamuffin," she declared like it was a fact you could look up. "Where did you ever get such a horrid haircut?"

She meant how short it was. When I'd lived with my aunt in Kansas, she cut it short as a boy's because she "didn't want to bother with it."

Winnie reached up and yanked a handful of my red hair.

"Ow!" I cried out. "Leggo, Winnie!"

She let loose of my hair but still clung to my arm. "And your eyes. They're the color of dirt, aren't they? Like those dirty people you belong with."

Her words hurt. Why would she be so mean? I tried to pull free, but Winnie's strength surprised me. She hung on.

"And those clothes," Winnie teased. Suddenly she frowned at me and pressed her hand to her lips. "Wait a minute. Something's wrong. You need . . . hmmm." Gripping my overalls strap, she yanked hard. I heard a rip and watched the button fly across the room.

My fists clenched tight, I wanted to sock that girl. But I wouldn't. I was raised proper.

Winnie released me and jumped back. "Perfect!" she exclaimed. "Now you really look your part, ragamuffin!"

She skipped back to the couch and collapsed laughing.

I flung open the trailer door and plunged outside. I wanted to get as far away from this foul child star as possible. But before I took off, I yelled, "You are a spiteful little brat, Winnie Collins! *And I don't care if you never come back to the set!*"

Chapter 5

No sooner had I shouted those words when I ran smack into Mr. Dixon. He stood with his fists clenched, scowling at me something fierce. Behind him, Tom looked none too happy. I felt my face grow hot and not from the blazing sun. I hung my head and studied my shoes.

"Correct me if I'm wrong, young lady," Mr. Dixon said, "but didn't Tom send for you so you could be a friend to Winnie?"

I glanced at the director. He pulled out his pocket watch and consulted it. Then, letting the watch dangle by its long, gold chain, he yanked off his safari hat and threw it down. It hit the dirt and spun around, reminding me of a model I'd once seen of the planet Saturn.

The two ant feeler hairs atop Mr. Dixon's red head quivered like they might burst into flame. He exploded with a terrible scream. "I am surrounded by total *incompetence!*"

Fetching the director's hat, Tom said sheepishly, "You got no call to blame Jessie here. It's our star. She—"

"It doesn't matter now," Mr. Dixon said, disgusted. "My goose is cooked. I'm already getting ten threatening telegrams a day from the studio. Everyone wants my head on a platter. I'm shutting us down. Tom, you and this girl can just find your own way back to California. If you need me, look me up in the bread lines."

"Mr. Dixon, please . . . let me explain," I begged.

Snatching his hat from Tom's hand, he growled, "You've said quite enough already, thank you."

With that, he stormed away.

We watched him until he disappeared. Then Tom shrugged. "I reckon we'd best head back to the hotel, missy."

I wanted to tell Tom and even Mr. Dixon that I'd tried to make friends with Winnie Collins. But that girl was pure cantankerous and downright mean. I tried to think of the right words to make Tom understand as I trailed him toward the edge of the settlement where he'd parked the car.

After a while Tom looked back and said, "Missy, I'm sorry I brought you all the way out here." His shoulders slumped and his face looked old and worried. At that instant I knew how bad I'd failed. Now, thanks to me and Winnie Collins, Tom was out of a job.

I couldn't bear to look straight at him. "I'm sorry too," I said. "I let you down. It's just that that girl got me so angry—"

"No need to explain, missy," he said. "I should've knowed you couldn't soften that little viper. I've met scorpions with sweeter dispositions."

The sun hovered straight up in the sky and scalded

everything below. I felt sweat drip off my face and run in streams down my shirt. All around us men scurried, packing equipment away in boxes. It looked like Mr. Dixon meant what he'd said.

We passed the town kids still hanging around. I saw Cap McCall and the red-haired boy standing together. The redhead shuffled up beside me and kicked sand over my shoes.

"We heard you yellin' at Winnie Collins," he said, his bottom lip stuck out. "If the movie company leaves, it really louses things up for our town, I'll have ya know. An' it's all *your* fault."

"Knock it off, Red," Cap told him.

But Red stood his ground. "*You* knock it off, Cap. Someone's gotta tell her off. My ma and pa was supposed to be extras in the train scene tomorrow. An' get paid for it too. Now they get nothin'."

It didn't make sense that I was to blame for all their troubles, and I wanted to set him straight. But I held back. In a way, I did feel responsible. After all, I hadn't convinced Winnie to finish her scenes. And now it seemed the moving picture company was shutting down.

"You know him?" Tom asked, pulling me away from the hostile boy.

"He's just some kid from town," I mumbled.

At the edge of the settlement Tom stopped suddenly. He grabbed my shoulder and looked me clean in the eyes. "Listen, missy, I just had a thought. Think you can walk back to the hotel from here? It's less than a mile." He pointed. "See it? Off thataway?"

"Sure, I can walk," I said. "But what about you?"

"I need to speak to Mr. Dixon. I don't know. Maybe he'll change his mind and decide to stay. Go on now. Just check into the hotel and wait for me there. OK?"

I doubted Tom could say anything to change Mr. Dixon's mind. These moving picture folks seemed a headstrong lot. But I nodded at Tom anyway and he hustled off.

* * *

By the time I reached the hotel, my shirt clung to me like a wet second skin. Mostly though, my head hurt from thinking about everything that had happened since I first stepped off the train. How I had seemingly brought an end to *Danger at Outlaw Creek*. How I'd lost Tom his job. And how—according to Red—I'd even brought trouble to Flintrock. Bringing disaster on folks gave me a rotten feeling.

I opened the hotel's creaky front door and stepped in. Compared to the hot brightness, the dark inside felt wonderfully cool. A ceiling fan rattled and stirred up dusty air.

When my eyes adjusted to the dim light, I glanced around the small lobby. In one corner sat a clay pot containing a tall, half dead cactus. A large painting of a desert scene hung over a long, lumpy couch. A metal floor lamp stood next to the couch, its faint light making a yellow oval on the wall. Off to the right a wide staircase led upstairs. A tall, thin man with a gray face slouched behind a wooden desk. He appeared to doze off even while standing up.

I went up to the desk. The man didn't seem to notice me. " 'Scuse me," I said.

He opened his eyes slightly.

"Yes?" he said dully. It struck me he resembled those desert lizards I'd seen sleeping on hot rocks.

"I'm supposed to have a room here," I told him.

"Oh? Your name?"

"Jessie Land."

He shuffled through some papers in front of him. I waited. When I heard the front door open, I glanced back.

I nearly gasped as I recognized the large man from the trailer. What had that woman—that Iola—called him? B.J.? He felt his way along the wall to the staircase like his eyes hadn't yet adjusted to the dark lobby. I noticed he held a brown paper sack bunched in his hand. I didn't trust the man, and I kept my eyes on him as he crept up the stairs.

"Ah, here we go," the lizard-man said. "Sign here."

He pushed a large book across the desk at me. I wrote my name. Then he handed me a key and two thin towels.

"Second floor," he said drowsily. "Next to last door on the right, room 29."

I stuck the towels under my arm and hurried for the stairs. I wanted to see what the man, B.J., was up to.

I crept up the stairs, staying well back. At the top I pressed myself back into a small alcove. Then leaning out,

I spied B.J. stepping carefully down the hall. Scratching his head, he knocked his derby hat askew. He paused at each door then went on, like he was looking for a particular room.

From my hiding place I watched B.J. stop at the last door. When he turned to look in my direction, I jerked back, hoping he hadn't seen me.

Peeking again, I saw him stick something into the door's lock. I heard him fumble with it. Then a click. He looked my way again and I dodged back.

When I peeked again, he'd already disappeared inside. I knew from his sneaky behavior that the room he'd entered didn't belong to him. So what could he be up to?

I tiptoed down the hall, stopping at number 29. My room. B.J. had entered the room at the end, right next to mine. Tom's room? I unlocked my door and quietly entered the room. I threw the towels on the narrow iron bed and went back to the door.

Holding it open a crack, I peeked out and waited for B.J. After the longest time, he came out of the room and in a moment went down the stairs.

I hurried out into the hall and noticed the sneaky villain had left the door open. Just like at the trailer.

I stepped inside the small room and looked around. It had a narrow iron bed like mine. A scarred chest of drawers stood near the only window where curtains flapped, drawing the hot and dusty air into the room. On the other side of the window sat a spindly looking chair, a small table, and a washstand with a white pitcher and bowl beneath a cracked mirror. Beside the mirror a sign informed me that the bathroom was down the hall. A long, ratty curtain hung over a doorway, which I took to be to the closet.

The only luggage in the room was a large satchel of cracked brown leather which I recognized as Tom's. Had B.J. taken anything?

I opened the satchel. Inside, I found Tom's clothes and personal things neatly arranged. I doubted B.J. had rifled through them. I checked the musty-smelling drawers in the chest. Empty. Pulling aside the curtain to the closet, I discovered nothing, only dust and a stack of yellowed newspapers.

It just didn't make sense to me. Why would that scoundrel break into Tom's room? I thought back to the conversation I'd overheard on the trailer steps. What exactly had B.J. and that Iola lady said? Something about Tom seeing Iola. But seeing her do what? Then I remembered one thing clearly. Iola had said they would "take care of" Tom soon. I'd meant to warn Tom but had forgotten all about it with the hubbub over Winnie.

Then I remembered something else. The brown paper sack that B.J. clutched in his hand when he came into the hotel. I didn't recall seeing him carry it when he left. Did he leave it behind? Here in Tom's room?

I checked out the window. Nothing on the narrow ledge.

I peered under the bed.

Stuck near the wall amid the dust balls I spied the sack.

I stretched under and retrieved it.

Sitting on the bed, I tested the sack's weight. Not much.

Then I dumped the contents onto the bed. *Money!* A heap of ten and twenty dollar bills. With shaking hands I stacked up the bills and counted them.

Two-hundred-fifty dollars.

Normally, I would take finding money to be good fortune. But this money smelled like trouble. Bad trouble.

Chapter 6

For a good long time I sat on the bed, looking at the money. I tried to make sense of it, but questions kept popping into my head. Why would B.J. hide all that money in Tom's room? There had to be some kind of shady business going on. Maybe the hidden money had to do with Iola's plan to "take care of" Tom.

I decided right then to show Tom the money and tell him what I'd seen. Maybe he'd have some answers.

I scooped the money back into the sack and left the room. I dreaded the long, hot trek back to the moving picture camp, but I had to find Tom.

By the time I tromped up to the parked studio vehicles, I felt plumb wore out. Sweat soaked my face, my shirt, even the paper sack I clutched tight. I noticed the kids from town still sitting in the sand. I tried to take a route around them, hoping to avoid meeting up with that red-head again.

When I entered the camp, I saw plenty of activity but no packing up.

Unfortunately, Red spied me. He trotted up and sneered, "If it ain't Miss High and Mighty."

He planted himself in front of me, his arms folded over

his chest. I noticed his grimy hands and fingernails. He seemed even tougher than before.

" 'Scuse me," I said, trying to walk around him, but he sidestepped me.

"Things got a heap better 'round here with you gone," he sassed. "Word is, Winnie went back to work. No thanks to you, of course. So why doncha just go back to wherever you come from and leave us alone?"

I had a mind to tell him what I thought of his rudeness, but his other words hit me.

"Did you say Winnie went back to work?" I asked.

He nodded. The way he stood there put me in mind of some sort of guard. Did he think he was protecting Winnie from the likes of me?

Fact was, I didn't care a whit what Winnie did. But I did care about Tom. I needed to find him and warn him about B.J. and the money and about the plot I'd overheard earlier.

At that moment Cap McCall came up.

"Leave her alone, Red."

His remark threw the tall boy off guard just long enough that I managed to push by him and dash into the crowd.

"Hey!" Red yelled after me.

I weaved through stacks of wooden crates and dodged men and women, some in costume, who tramped about. Nearer the set, I stepped over a sea of cords and cables that hooked up the cameras and lights. I spotted Mr. Dixon talking to Winnie in front of the blacksmith's shop.

She wore her costume and wig and held the script in her hand. Red was right. Winnie had gone back to work.

I looked around for Tom. No sign of him. Then, farther off I saw dust rising and heard the whinny of horses. I headed that way.

At the edge of the street scene I came upon a small corral. Five men in chaps and boots and cowboy hats leaned against the crude fence. But these weren't real cowboys. They wore makeup on their faces and their hands looked soft and pink, not like Daddy's. He worked on a real ranch and his tanned hands felt rough from hard work. The fake cowboys stood gazing at the horses dancing about inside the corral. In the middle of the corral I spied Tom leading an Appaloosa toward the men.

"Tom!" I cried, clutching the paper sack tight.

He squinted at me and looked puzzled.

I scrambled between the rough boards of the corral and ran over to him.

"I've gotta talk to you," I exclaimed.

"Missy, I thought you went to the hotel," he said.

"I did, and I saw that B.J. character," I began.

"You speakin' of B.J. Seeds?" he asked.

"I guess so. Who is he anyway?"

"He works for Iola Linville. She's Mr. Dixon's assistant and the bookkeeper. B.J.'s sweet on her."

I considered this information a moment then said, "I saw him in town and—"

"Listen, missy," Tom interrupted, "Can we talk later? Winnie's come back to work, so we're makin' up for lost time. I've gotta show these fellas somethin' about horses."

"But Tom," I said, "that B.J., he—"

"Wait, missy. I gotta get this done first. Meet me at the canteen when we break for lunch. You can tell me all about it then."

He pointed toward a row of tables and benches beneath the shade of a large sheet of canvas. A couple of women busied themselves laying out food on a table.

I nodded. I sure didn't want to do anything else to cause Tom trouble.

I climbed out of the corral and walked over to the canteen. Though past noon, no one was eating. I sat on one of the rough benches, still clutching the crumpled, still damp paper sack. Even in the shade the heat hung on me like a heavy coat. A light breeze stirred up the dust and blew it around some but didn't help cool the air. I shut my eyes and thought about home. I imagined the fresh air blowing in Santa Monica. In my mind I saw Mama and Daddy on the porch of our new house. My heart ached for them.

"Why did I ever come to this place?" I said softly to myself.

"A very good question, dear," came a familiar voice.

I jerked. Opening my eyes, I looked directly into the face of none other than Iola Linville. She and B.J. Seeds stood not five feet away, staring right at me. For a moment I froze. Then I realized she wasn't really staring at me but at what I held. Her eyes were fixed on the paper sack.

Iola gave B.J. a quick, mean glance. She didn't say a word, but I could read her thoughts.

And so could B.J. He scratched his head and said, "I *did* put it under the old man's bed."

I got up slow, my muscles tight, ready to spring in any direction. I tightened my grip on the sack.

"Tom!" I squeaked as Iola and B.J. closed in on me.

I rushed over to the ladies laying out food.

"Please," I cried. "Help me. Those—"

One of the ladies looked up, waved a finger at me, and threatened, "I told you town kids to stay outta this canteen. We feed the movie company and no one else."

At that moment the villains closed in on me. I darted between the canteen ladies and ran as fast as I could. I cut right, then left, and raced past three women in red, frilly dresses. I leaped over a locker heaped full of black electrical cords and scooted behind something covered with yellow canvas. I collapsed to the ground, my breath heaving, my heart thundering in my chest. I felt like I had used up every ounce of strength I had. Peeking out of my hiding place, I spotted Iola only a few feet away. She had stopped to talk to a woman in red.

Too close! I tightened my grip on the sack, sprang up, and took off.

I heard B.J. yell, *"There she goes!"*

The heavy stomp of his feet kept me running. I bumped into a man dressed in black. A mask covered his eyes. He muttered, "Watch it, little lady."

Then, all of a sudden, I found myself at the row of

trailers. I glanced back. No, I couldn't see them, not yet anyway. Somehow I knew I couldn't let them get the sack. I had to hide it. Thinking quickly, I tossed it under the closest trailer. It rolled a bit and settled in a patch of weeds. *Good,* I thought. *I'd get it later.*

Then I heard Iola's sugary sweet voice sing out. "No need to worry. She can't hide from us." I knew she must be nearby, even though I couldn't see her yet.

I thought of running to the town kids. Maybe Cap McCall would help me. But I couldn't take a chance with that Red around.

I heard voices coming closer. I needed to hide—and fast! I glanced around. The silver trailers gleamed in the sunlight, hurting my eyes. *Winnie's trailer!* I'd seen her on the set and knew it was empty. I could hide there.

I rushed over to Winnie's trailer and yanked on the door.

Locked!

I ran to the next trailer. Locked too!

At the door to the third trailer, I hesitated. Please, God....

The knob turned in my hand. I lunged inside, closing the door quickly behind me. Whew! I stood still a moment, catching my breath. Everything in the dark trailer seemed to be spinning. I shut my eyes and rubbed my hot forehead.

When I opened my eyes again, I saw a desk with a small lamp on it. I spied papers lying about. A box heaped full of clothes sat in one corner. The air carried a familiar scent. Perfume. Wait a minute. . . .

This must be Iola's trailer!

Behind me, on the other side of the door, came voices.

"Don't worry, Iola sugar, we'll find her," B.J. said.

"I'm not worried," she snapped. "And I've told you a hundred times. Stop calling me 'sugar'!"

Their feet sounded as they climbed the wooden steps. Oh, no!

Chapter 7

I dashed for the desk and dived beneath it. Huddled there on a scratchy purple rug, I made myself as small and as still as possible. "Please don't let them see me hiding here," I prayed silently.

Then I heard the trailer door creak open and the stomp of feet. I held my breath and my mouth went dry as cotton. Why did I pick this trailer? What if I got trapped here for hours? Or worse—got found out!

I heard Iola say, "We must get that sack back, B.J. Do you understand me? That child must have seen you plant it in the old man's room. Do you realize what that means if she tells Walt? We had enough trouble with that old man before she ever showed up."

Since they had commenced talking in their normal voices, I figured they hadn't seen me. I took a deep breath and stretched out my fingers, trying to relax a bit. My hand touched something. I drew the object closer—a small black notebook. Then I remembered having seen an object fall from the desk that morning when I'd accidentally crashed through the door of the trailer. Was this what had fallen off the desk?

I heard someone pacing.

"Why doncha sit down and take it easy?" B.J. said.

Suddenly the chair beside the desk pulled away. I held my breath again, frozen in panic.

"Just tell me, B.J.," Iola said sharply, "how can I relax when I'm about to be found out?"

I heard Iola plop down in the chair.

"Things could be worse," B.J. said. The desk creaked and I realized he was sitting on the corner of it. I tried to make myself even smaller.

"You're really a source of comfort, B.J.," said Iola like she didn't mean a word of it. "But if you say, 'Things get darker just before the dawn,' I'll scream."

"That's an unhealthy attitude," replied B.J.

"OK. You tell me what could be worse than the fix we're in."

"Well, I don't think we need to worry about that girl. It's just the old man, Iola sugar. He probably knows you—"

"I *know* what he knows, idiot!" Iola barked. "And quit calling me 'sugar'!"

I tried to put the pieces of the puzzle together. Tom knew something damaging about Iola. He'd seen something she didn't want him to see. But what? And what did the sack of money have to do with it? I just couldn't fit the pieces in place.

I heard Iola get up and start pacing.

From farther off she said, "We've got to get rid of them—both of them. That's all there is to it."

I trembled at her words. *Get rid of them!* Did she mean

Tom and me? Dear Lord, help us. I had to get out of here. And I had to warn Tom. But how?

My fingers tightened on the black notebook. I slipped it into my pocket. Maybe it had something to do with these villains and their no-good plans.

Abruptly, Iola stopped pacing.

I heard her say, "Well, B.J. It's time to go."

"Huh?" the man replied.

"Let's *go,*" Iola repeated.

"But Iola sug—I mean, Iola. Where're we going?"

"You'll find out."

I heard him cross the floor. Then I heard the trailer door open and slam shut.

Were they truly gone? I forced myself to stay balled up under the desk a few minutes. Just in case.

When I couldn't stand it a moment longer, I crawled out from under the desk.

When I stood up, I saw them. Iola's white clothes caught my eye first. B.J. stood beside her holding his hat and scratching his head. She smiled like a cat that had just trapped a mouse. He frowned like he couldn't figure out where I'd come from.

I'd been found out!

Chapter 8

What else could I do? I plopped down in the chair beside the desk.

My mind raced from one awful thing to another. How would I ever get out of here and find Tom?

Iola moved toward me, taking small, catlike steps.

Then she seemed to tower over me, her eyes narrow slits. She grabbed my shoulder. "Just what did you hear?" she demanded, leaning closer. All at once I smelled her perfume. A strong, sweet, musty scent, like too many flowers. It put me in mind of a funeral I'd once attended with Mama and Daddy.

I had thought Iola Linville to be quite young when I'd seen her that morning. But closer up I noticed fine lines stretching out from her eyes and around her mouth. She wore a lot of face powder and had heavy black eyelashes. A strand of black hair spilled down over her unblinking, deep, green eyes and she shoved it back. Her gaze fixed on me. I had to look away.

"I asked you a question, dear," she said, a false sweetness to her voice.

"I didn't hear anything," I replied.

"You're a snoopy girl, aren't you? Two times today

you've eavesdropped on me and B.J."

Her charge irked me. "I'm no snoop."

"But you did sneak in here this morning, just like a thief," she accused. She leaned even closer, and the head of the poor dead critter around her neck swung right in front of my eyes. "What did you plan to steal?"

"As I recall, Iola, she more like fell in the door this morning," said B.J.

"Just shut up, B.J.," Iola spat at him, her gaze never leaving my face. "Only a snoop—or a thief—would hide under a person's desk."

"You were *chasing* me!" I protested.

Smiling slightly, she said in a soft, almost pleasant voice, "Ah yes. And why was that?"

I kept still.

"Where's that sack?" she demanded, her voice fierce.

At that moment I got fed up with her questions. Fed up with her mean look and her plotting, whatever it involved.

"You mean the sack that man hid in Tom's room?" I replied, pointing at B.J. "The sack with two-hundred-and-fifty dollars cash money in it?"

"The sack you *stole,*" Iola corrected me.

"I'll never tell you!" I fired back. "Never! You're up to no good. That much I know. And I intend to warn Tom and Mr. Dixon!"

Then she did something I didn't expect. She bent back and cackled with laughter.

Her strange behavior shook me. Shook me good. I tried to get up. She pushed me back down in the chair, her laughter ceasing at once.

"You're not going anywhere, dear, until you answer my questions," she said, shaking her finger in my face.

God forgive me but I wanted to bite it.

"I can see we'll have to start over," she said. "What did you do with that sack?"

"I forget," I said with a shrug.

"Well, we'll just have to help you remember," she threatened. "Right, B.J.?"

He muttered something.

She leaned closer. The dead creature brushed against my cheek. I cringed. "Why did that old man send for you?"

"I don't appreciate your calling him 'that old man,' " I told her. "His name is Tom McCauley."

Her eyebrows shot up. "Yes. McCauley. I've heard he's got a checkered past."

"Tom may've been in prison, but he paid his debt in full," I said in defense of my friend. "He's reformed. And he's a better—" I stopped short, realizing suddenly that I'd said too much.

"Prison, eh?" Iola said, smiling slyly. "Well, do tell. So why did he send for you? And why have you been snooping around me and B.J.?"

"I can't answer your questions when you throw them at me all at once," I told her, still regretting what I'd let slip about Tom.

"You *are* going pretty fast with the questions, Iola sugar," B.J. observed.

"Shut up, B.J. This girl—"

A knock at the door interrupted her. Iola froze. Standing beside the door, B.J. scratched his head like he couldn't decide what to do. His hat fell off and rolled around his feet. I saw my chance to cry for help.

But the instant I opened my mouth Iola's hand came up to cover it. I struggled, trying to scream, trying to get out of the chair.

"B.J., over here!" she ordered.

From outside a man yelled, "Iola, you in there?"

B.J. hurried over to us.

"Keep her quiet," Iola told him.

He pulled out a handkerchief, wrapped it around his hand, and clamped it over my mouth. Iola pulled away.

"She might have germs," he remarked.

The doorknob turned! I struggled against B.J., but I was no match for him.

"Iola?" came the voice as the door began to open.

Iola lurched, reaching the door before the man could get a glimpse inside the trailer.

"What do you want?" she huffed.

"Lunch time," the man called out. "And I oughta warn you—Walt's on the warpath looking for you. Oh, and they're setting the dynamite charge for the bank robbery scene."

"Be right out," she answered through the crack in the door.

Then, slamming the door shut, she turned and squinted at me, her hands on her hips.

"What about that sack of money?" B.J. said to her, his hand still over my mouth.

"Not now, B.J.," she said flatly. "I've got to go. You keep her here, you understand? I'll be back soon."

"Can you bring me some lunch, sug—?" he asked.

Iola groaned, "Oh, you dolt!" Then she went out.

B.J. took his hand away from my mouth and shook out his handkerchief. I wiped my mouth on my shirt sleeve.

"You've no call to hold me like a prisoner," I told him.

He said, "You just stay quiet, girl. Unless you care to tell me where you hid that sack."

I didn't say a word. He pulled a stool over to the door and settled himself on it. He put me in mind of a circus elephant perched on a box.

* * *

Time passed and neither of us spoke. B.J. paid me no mind. He took his derby off and peered at it. He scratched his head about ten times. Once he got up and turned on the radio. I sat in the chair, tapping my foot and thinking. I needed a plan. A plan for escaping this trailer and B.J.

I remembered something he had said and done earlier. And an idea came to me.

I cleared my throat and started in, "You know, this dry climate here really appeals to reptiles."

B.J. frowned. "What are you talking about?"

"Snakes. I'm talking about snakes."

He cringed.

I went on. "Haven't you noticed how people out here mostly wear boots?"

He shook his head.

"It's because they don't want to get bitten on the ankle," I explained, doubting if one soul in Flintrock even owned a pair of boots. So far I'd only seen barefoot children.

B.J. bent over, lifted his pant leg, and gazed at his dark socks. He looked back at me. I saw worry haunting his eyes. Then his face relaxed a bit.

"You don't know what you're talking about."

"Oh, but I do," I said in my most grown-up voice. I swallowed hard, knowing I'd have to tell a bold-faced lie or my plan didn't have a chance. "I saw two men over by the corral catch a big diamondback snake longer than your arm. A *rattler!*"

B.J. stiffened. He leaned back against the door. "A rattlesnake?" he asked, his eyes large.

"Winnie Collins herself told me she found a nest of rattlers in her trailer," I said. "Baby ones."

"What?" he gasped.

"Sure," I insisted. "Somehow the mama got inside and laid her eggs and had nine or ten baby snakes, just like that."

"I never heard that."

I shrugged. "Well, I'll bet you didn't know that the babies are more poisonous than the grown ones. The poison's more—more—concentrated in them. Plus they can get in places the big ones can't . . . like up your pant leg."

I stooped over and shook out my pant leg as though I'd just felt something crawl up it. I watched as B.J. hopped up and did the same.

"Girl, what was that you said about snakes this morning when you sprang in here?" he asked.

Just the chance I'd been waiting for! I gasped and widened my eyes. Then I sprang to my feet and glanced around.

"Oh gosh no!" I cried. "I plumb forgot."

"Forgot what?" the big man demanded.

"That snake—the one I saw slither in here," I said. "You left the door open and I saw it."

"What?"

"It's true," I lied. "Please, don't make me sit over here all alone. Please. I'm deathly afraid of snakes."

"You are?" he replied, shivering and looking about. "Come over here. Maybe we oughta step outside to wait for Iola."

As I crossed the room, I pointed and shouted, *"There!* There it is!"

"Where?" he shrieked. He backed flat against the door, knocking his derby to the floor and blocking my escape. I had to get him away.

"There—by the door!" I cried, pointing at his feet.

I'd never seen such a big man leap like that. He bounded past me and tripped over the box of clothes.

My chance! I shot to the door, turned the knob, and yanked it open.

Glancing back, I saw B.J. clambering to his feet. A

cowboy shirt covered his head and a black skirt dangled from his arm. He yelled, *"Awk!* Girl, where'd it go? Where's that snake?"

"By your foot!" I cried. Then I hopped through the doorway, skidded down the two steps, and landed on my knees on the ground. A cloud of brown dust puffed up around me.

No sooner had I scrambled to my feet than B.J. appeared in the door, the cowboy shirt clenched in his fist. His angry face told me he no longer believed my snake story. He jumped down to the ground, his enormous hands fumbling for me.

I dodged him and ran between the trailers and a row of trucks.

B.J. gasped, "Slow down, girl, I'd like a word with you!"

I ducked under a truck and rolled to the other side. Then I crawled through a maze of boxes and equipment piled high. Up ahead I spotted the back of the phony sheriff's office and storefronts. The set! Tom might be over there.

I jumped to my feet and dashed away.

At the back of the storefronts, I dropped to the ground again. I crawled through a tangle of boxes, working my way to the front side of the wooden set. Then I hid, relieved, behind a large stack of crates.

I heard a voice cry out, "Clear the set!"

I stuck my head up a little and spotted B.J. nearby, still looking for me. He faced the other direction and scratched his head. I ducked back down behind the crates. Maybe if I stayed put, I'd be safe.

After a moment I peeked out again. B.J. had turned and stared right at me! He smiled. Then he headed my way!

Dear Lord, please protect me, I prayed, my eyes shut tight.

When I looked again, there stood B.J. His smile had disappeared and alarm showed on his face. He shook his head and started to back away. His mouth opened and closed like he wanted to shout something, but no words came out.

Then I heard the cry, *"All clear! Quiet! Action!"*

At that instant I looked at the rough, wooden boxes surrounding me. Stamped on them were two words in large black letters:

DANGER–EXPLOSIVES!

Suddenly it all made perfect sense. B.J.'s fearful look. Explosives! They were about to blow up the set with dynamite! I had to get away!

I shot out from my hiding place and ran, fast as I could, toward the cameras.

"Wait, wait!" I yelled. *"Don't blow me up!"*

But the blast ignited behind me. The earth shook and a deafening roar burst in my ears. I pitched high into the air like a bundle of dry sticks. Fire and light flashed around me.

Then everything went from red to black.

Chapter 9

Layers and layers of dusty gauze lifted from my eyes. Light slowly filtered in.

So this was heaven.

A bright, white light hurt my eyes, but I looked anyway. In the middle of the light sat a gray-haired man. My guardian angel, I realized at once.

His name was Tom, I knew that much.

Then the light faded and I slipped back into a dark, dark place.

* * *

When the light returned, I forced myself to hold on to it. To use it as a way to pull myself out of the darkness.

I made out a sky of dingy, white plaster. No, a ceiling. This was a room. Behind my head a bar of iron, most of the brown paint worn off. Above that, upside down, a building. No, a photograph of a building. Written in fancy script across the gray sky were words. I didn't read them. It hurt my head to try. My eyes drifted to another wall with a ratty cardboard sign stuck on it. I worked hard to read those words because they were big and black and right side up.

NO SPITTING ON THE FLOOR

My eyes wanted to roll back into my head and carry me back to wherever I'd come from. But I blinked and forced myself to stay awake.

Heat hovered around me in the room, making it hard to breathe. I looked at the wall again. Beside the sign light flooded in. A window. The faded blue curtains stirred, but I felt no air.

A man sat in a chair in the light, leaning out like he wanted to catch the breeze. An elderly man, tall even when he sat, with a sun-reddened face and steel gray hair and a white moustache and a splash of white beard. Dressed in a faded purple shirt and black trousers. Dusty green boots.

An angel?

His name came floating out of memory.

"Tom?" I spoke with a strange, croaking voice.

The man jerked and shot up from the chair. In two strides he stood by my side.

"Missy," he said, his eyes watering. His wrinkled face smiled down at me.

He sat on the edge of the bed and put his warm, dry hand on my forehead. I closed my eyes, the urge still strong to drift back.

I told myself, *stay here. Don't go back.*

"Missy," Tom said gently, "how do you feel?"

I opened my eyes.

Once he asked, I realized my whole body hurt. My legs, my arms, my head. Most of all, my poor head.

"Like an ache with skin," I told him.

He chuckled.

"Where am I?" I asked.

"Your hotel room," he replied. "We got you here right after the explosion. The studio's makeup lady put you to bed."

Explosion?

"The doc here in town he gave you the once-over," Tom explained in a soft voice. "Said if you come to, if you called me by name. . . . " He stopped, like he couldn't bring himself to finish.

"What happened?" I said.

"Don't you remember?"

I thought back, through all the layers of dusty gauze and darkness. My brain ached as I fought to recall something, *anything*. Scraps of things—a bratty girl with a towel wrapped around her head, a red-haired boy with his lip stuck out—jerked around in my head.

I felt tears stream from the corners of my eyes. I tasted their saltiness on my lips.

Tom's hand came up and wiped my face with a rag.

"Don't cry, missy. The main thing is you're OK. Leastwise you look OK."

"What happened?" I asked again.

"Well, you came runnin' out from behind some crates they was all set to blow up in the bank robbery scene," he explained. "Fact is, it did blow up and you went a-sailin'. Hit the ground like a load of bricks and got knocked out cold."

When I didn't say anything, he leaned closer and asked, "Can you tell me your name, missy?"

I spoke right up. "Jessie Land."

"And where are you?"

"Flintrock, Arizona. Visiting you on a moving picture set."

"And what's the picture called?"

"Danger at Outlaw Creek," I answered, surprised I could recall.

He leaned back and let go a sigh. "I thought there for a minute you couldn't remember nothin'."

"But there *is* something I'm not remembering," I told him. I put my hand to my head and rubbed gently. "It hurts too much or I'd try to think harder. There's . . . something . . . something I needed to warn *you* about."

Tom took my hand and patted it. "Don't you fret 'bout nothin', missy. We just gotta get you well."

Another name drifted into my mind. "Mr. Dixon," I said.

"Mr. Dixon?" Tom shook his head. "Well, he pitched his hat plenty far after that blast, believe you me. He thought you ruined his shot. I figured he was gonna explode himself till the cameramen told him you weren't in the way when the dynamite blew."

"I mean . . . I mean," I began, struggling to say just what I did mean. "There's something I need to tell him too."

"Well, don't you worry. It'll come to you in good time. Meanwhile, you hungry?"

"No," I said. "I mean, yes. I mean, maybe."

Tom laughed. "Well, you should be. It's after supper time and you never even ate lunch. Tell you what. I'll go get you some vittles and you can decide when you see 'em if you're hungry. How 'bout that?"

I nodded.

He stood up. "Just get some rest. I'll be back soon's I can."

"OK."

He went out. I closed my eyes and drifted off again, feeling better just knowing that when I opened them again Tom would be there.

* * *

When I woke, the bright light was gone. The room lay wrapped in darkness. The quietness alarmed me. I sat up. When I did, a sharp pain jabbed in my head, like someone had rapped it smartly with a hammer. I stayed on the edge of the bed for a spell, holding my head in my hands and breathing slowly in and out. That helped some.

I worked my way around the bed and made it to the wall. Then I ran my hands over the cracked surface, feeling for the light switch. I found it and flipped it on. The light burst on like a tiny explosion. I covered my eyes for a time, letting them adjust.

Then, when I looked around, I had only one question.

Where was Tom?

I went to the washstand to splash some water on my face. Standing in front of the mirror I gasped and jumped back. *Who on earth—?* But the short red hair and brown eyes alerted me. The reflection belonged to me, all right. What I hadn't been prepared for were all the scratches and bruises. I splashed my face with water. It stung something fierce. I made sure not to look in the mirror again.

In the closet I found my suitcase and dug out a clean shirt and underwear. I dressed quickly. The broken strap of my overalls brought Winnie Collins' face to mind. But my thoughts didn't linger on her. I fixed the strap with a safety pin I found in the chest of drawers. Then I took the dirty overalls, turned them upside down, and gave them a good shake. Dust puffed up in my face.

Something struck my foot. I looked down and saw a small black notebook on the floor. Where did that come from?

I pulled on my overalls and sat in the rickety chair. I flipped through the notebook's pages, trying to remember. I saw numbers. Columns and columns of numbers and dollar signs on every page.

At once a memory shook loose. The paper sack of money hid under Tom's bed. I even remembered counting it—two-hundred-fifty dollars.

Then, one right after another, the memories came back, falling into place like puzzle pieces.

B.J. stashing the sack of money under Tom's bed.

Busting in on Iola and B.J. in a trailer.

Hiding under a desk and finding the notebook.

Iola and B.J. trapping me in the trailer, asking me loads of questions.

B.J. chasing me through the moving picture camp.

Hiding again, then reading those awful words, *DANGER—EXPLOSIVES!* I shuddered. I wouldn't remember the rest. I just wouldn't.

Then one more memory jolted me. A voice. I'd heard Iola Linville say, *"The old man we'll take care of soon. Maybe tonight."*

I glanced out the window. A single street light glowed in the dark, empty street. From far away came muffled booms. Thunder? I thought I saw lightning crackle in the distance. But my mind fixed on Tom. Where was he? I had failed to warn him about Iola and B.J. and their plot against him, whatever it was. I feared he'd met up with danger.

I shot to my feet. The sudden movement caused my head to pound. I staggered. Dizzy, I reached out and grabbed hold of the chairback. *Whew!* Getting blown up sure takes its toll on a person.

I remembered Tom in my room. Beside me. Then leaving to get me something to eat. Surely that had been hours ago. Somehow in my heart I knew. He was in danger.

I still clutched the black notebook. I didn't understand how it fit into this puzzle, but I knew it must be important. Lifting up the mattress, I stuck the notebook underneath. Then I went out into the dimly lit hall and locked the door behind me. I saw no one about as I went down the stairs.

In the lobby, a man sat behind the desk. His head nodded as he dozed in the chair.

A clock in the lobby chimed twelve times. Midnight. I went to the front door. What could have become of Tom?

As I looked out the window, I saw someone standing alone under the street light. Something about him seemed familiar, and I pressed my nose against the glass. He wore a floppy cap and a pair of ragged-looking trousers and no shoes.

All at once his name danced in my memory—Cap McCall. While the other town kids, especially the one named Red, had treated me bad, Cap seemed almost friendly.

I pushed open the door and rushed across the street.

When he looked up and saw me, he jumped back. *"What?"* he cried. "Where'd *you* come from?"

"It's me," I told him, "Jessie Land."

"I know who you are," he replied, staring hard at me. "But I heard you got yourself blowed up. In fact, you kinda *look* like you got yourself blowed up."

I put my hand to my face. I knew I looked a sight. Wanting to change the subject, I asked, "What're you doing about at this hour?"

"Pop's workin' late at the garage," he replied, still staring at me. He leaned closer and took another good look. Satisfied, he stepped back and explained, "He's gotta get a car fixed for that Mr. Dixon by morning."

"Listen, Cap, have you seen my friend?" I asked. "Tom McCauley?"

He just stared at me. Then he took off his cap and squeezed it in his hands. His bad haircut looked worse under the street light.

"What's the matter, boy?" I said. "Do you know something about Tom?"

"You talkin' 'bout the *old* guy? With the white moustache and the black hat?"

"That's the one," I said. "You seen him?"

"You haven't heard, I take it."

"Heard what?"

I stared at Cap, a horrible fear trembling through me. Wanting to know what had happened to Tom and yet not wanting to know at the same time.

"He got hisself into a heap a trouble. Stole somethin' from Mr. Dixon's what I hear. The police chief's got him locked up in jail."

Chapter 10

"Jail!" I exclaimed. "But Tom's no thief."

Cap shrugged.

I stared into the boy's freckled face. We stood in the glow of the street light. Bugs buzzed in my face, but I didn't wave them off. My head still ached from the explosion, but now my heart ached worse. Tom in jail? Accused of stealing? Cap's words just didn't make sense.

The boy kicked at the dusty brick street with his bare foot. "Seems he was a thief once. Spent time in prison. Iola said so herself."

"Iola! But what does she know . . . ?"

It hit me. She knew about Tom's criminal past because I'd told her. No doubt she told Mr. Dixon and the police too. So Tom's being in jail was my fault. I had to go see him, to get him free.

I asked Cap where I could find the jail.

"I'll go with ya," he offered.

"Thanks, but I'd best take care of this myself."

He turned away, like I'd hurt his feelings. I wanted to do something to make it up to him. To show that I liked and trusted him. I remembered the black leather notebook.

I pulled my room key from my pocket. "Here," I said,

"take this."

"What—?"

"The key to my room. Number 29. Under the mattress you'll find a black notebook. Fetch it and give it to Mr. Dixon, OK? It's very important."

He smiled at me. "Sure! I'll do it, Jessie." Then he pointed down the street and said, "Go right after ya pass the dentist's office. Jail's on the next block over. Can't miss it. Gotta a green light out front."

I stuck my hand out and said, "Thanks, Cap."

He eyed my hand carefully, then shook it.

As I headed toward the police station, thoughts buzzed in my head like the bugs around the street lamp. I had to get Tom out of jail. But how? I knew he wouldn't steal anything from Mr. Dixon. Cap had mentioned Iola. Probably she was behind the whole thing. Probably—

Oh, no!

I stopped. How did Cap know Iola? *Fool girl! You trusted him without even thinking.* Would he really give the notebook to Mr. Dixon? Already I began to doubt my newfound friend.

But thinking these things just hurt my head worse. First I needed to see Tom. Then I could worry about Cap and the notebook.

When I passed the dentist's office and turned right, I thought I heard voices. I looked back for Cap, but he had disappeared. I hurried down the dark street, spying a green light on a building far ahead.

I sped past several old buildings with FORECLOSED or

OUT OF BUSINESS or BUSTED signs in the windows. I noticed three automobiles parked in the street, two without tires. *Flintrock, the town that Roosevelt forgot,* I thought.

I got a strange feeling, like someone lurked nearby. I stopped and spun around. No one. *Of course not, you're being silly,* I told myself. Who would be out at this hour? I passed a shop window. A clock inside read twelve-thirty.

Finally, I stood beneath the green light on the wall of the Flintrock Police Station. A crude sign on the building said: Est. 1909.

Strange as it seemed, I thought I heard breathing. For a moment I stood still, wanting to turn and look behind me, but fearing to. I heard a car coming up the street.

As I turned toward the sound, everything went black. A thick, scratchy covering swept down over my head. What on earth—? I grabbed it, trying to push it off, but a pair of arms tightened around me.

"Hey!" I cried out. *"Hey! Lemme go!"*

The arms circled me tight. I tried to scream, but the cloth muffled my cries.

The car engine grew louder. I struggled, kicking at the strong person holding me. My legs only lashed out at the air. I heard the automobile stop. A door opened.

A rough shove sent me sprawling inside the car. I rolled off the seat and got wedged on the floor. A hand grabbed me, yanked me back to the seat, and held me still.

The car door slammed shut. The engine roared. I felt the car jerk. Carrying me off into the blackness.

Chapter 11

The moment my captor let go, I tore off the covering. My face stung as the thick, rough cloth rubbed against my scrapes and bruises. Light from the dashboard gave off a faint green glow in the car.

Behind the wheel, I spied none other than Iola Linville. In the back seat beside me sat B.J. Seeds. No surprise.

"Let me out of this vehicle," I demanded.

Iola glanced back, her face grim. "Where's my notebook?" she asked.

"Let me out *now,*" I insisted. "This's kidnapping!"

Her crazy laugh filled the car, filling me with anger and fear.

"I'll give you the notebook when you stop this car."

She stomped on the brake, throwing B.J. and me forward. B.J.'s hat flew off.

"Iola sugar, take it easy," B.J. remarked, pulling me back in the seat and fetching his hat from the floor.

The villain turned around and stretched out her hand. "All right, hand it over."

I looked at her long, thin fingers reaching toward my face, her pointed fingernails, painted red. I smelled the woman's flowery perfume. "I . . . I don't exactly have it on me," I stammered, pressing back in the seat. "But I can get it. Just take me back to the hotel."

"It's in your room?"

"No. I hid it." I thought of Cap and wondered if he'd retrieved the notebook yet. And if he had, what he'd do with it.

"Hid it where?" she demanded.

"I'll tell you," I said, "but not till you tell Mr. Dixon the truth about Tom. That he's no thief. That he doesn't belong in jail."

Her laugh exploded in the car again, setting off an explosion of pain in my head. It seemed loud enough to wake the whole town of Flintrock.

She turned to the front and tromped the gas pedal, propelling me back in my seat. "Gag her, B.J.," she yelled. "I don't wish to hear one more word out of her."

"Where are you taking me?" I cried as B.J. reached out to tie a handkerchief over my mouth. I batted his large hands away.

"Stop," I warned, "or I'll poke you in the eye."

The big man hesitated.

"B.J., just do it!" Iola shouted.

He leaned toward me. I tried to shove him back. But he was a bear of a man, and I couldn't budge him. He backed me into the corner of the seat and grabbed my hands. Then he snapped something cold and hard on my wrists. Handcuffs! In the green glow I saw his eyes. They looked kind of sad and sorrowful as he did the dirty deed.

When he took up the handkerchief again, I pleaded,

"Don't, B.J." He paused only an instant, then tied it tight around my mouth.

"Pretty good thinking bringing these prop handcuffs along, right, Iola?" B.J. said.

Iola stared silently ahead.

I struggled against the handcuffs and the gag, but it only tired me. I couldn't get free.

"Why doncha just relax and enjoy the ride, girl," B.J. said, patting my arm. "Doncha you think she oughta just relax and enjoy the ride, Iola?"

Iola didn't answer. She kept her attention on the dark road as the car sped farther away from Flintrock. I had no idea where we were headed, but we were getting there fast.

"Dear, if you'd only left well enough alone," Iola said after a while, "if you'd only minded your own business, you wouldn't be in this fix. Am I right or am I right, B.J.?"

"You're right, Iola," B.J. said. "This girl has been a particular pest to us, hasn't she?"

I glared at B.J. He smiled at me, sort of friendly like.

Iola made a sharp left turn and the road got rougher.

Staring out the window as the car rocked along, I saw nothing but dark land and dark sky, save an occasional flash of lightning. I cowered in the seat and tried to think. But the only thought that came to me was that this woman—Iola Linville—might do *any*thing.

We bounded over the rough road for the longest time. Finally the car slowed, then stopped. Iola rolled down her window and stared out at the darkness.

B.J. remarked, "Right pretty night out. Think maybe when we get back to town we can take us a little stroll?"

"You idiot, it's after one o'clock in the morning," complained Iola.

I heard the low rumble of distant thunder.

"My goodness, I hope it doesn't rain," B.J. said.

"There it is," Iola sang out, pointing through the window.

I tried to look, but whatever she saw was lost to me. As the car started up, I prayed. *Dear Lord, I'm afraid of these two. Afraid of what they're planning.*

The car swung right, then left. In the headlights I thought I could make out the shapes of buildings. A town?

"There 'tis, Iola, over that way," B.J. said.

"I see it for Pete's sake," she grumbled.

The car turned left again and stopped. I leaned forward. The headlights lit up a row of buildings. But something seemed strange. There were no lights anywhere, and the buildings reminded me of the moving picture set, only all old and worn down.

B.J. peered out the window up at the sky. "You know, Iola, I'm a little nervous about thunderstorms."

Iola swung around and gave him a harsh look. "These dumb remarks, B.J.—are they for real or are they just an act?"

His head dropped and he stared at his lap. For a moment I almost felt sorry for B.J. Seeds.

"You've got no call to treat me so nasty, Iola," he pouted. "I've done all you told me, haven't I?"

Iola reached out and patted his face almost playfully. "Yes, you have, B.J.," she said. "I couldn't have done this without you. So let's get it over with, all right?"

Get it over with! At those words, my stomach knotted up and my mouth went dry. Just what did she plan to do with me?

Iola climbed out of the car, leaving the engine running and the headlights on. B.J. opened his door and stepped out too. Then Iola opened my door.

"Get out," she ordered.

I scooted across to the other side, hoping to escape, but B.J. grabbed me by the straps of my overalls and yanked me back.

"Gotcha, girl!"

He took my arm and led me toward the crumbling building. I glanced left and right and saw other buildings just like it. The wooden walk in front had rotted and splintered. I kept thinking about the set of *Danger at Outlaw Creek.* Only this place was old and empty and falling down.

Iola pushed through the door to the building. B.J. dragged me in after her. The smell of dust hung heavy in the stale air. A cobweb snared my face and I jerked away. Phoo!

This was no movie set. We stood in a real room. Then I realized: *this must be the ghost town Tom made mention of!*

Iola struck a match and lit a kerosene lamp. The flickering light revealed a broken desk and three smashed chairs in the small space.

B.J. shoved me along and we followed Iola down a narrow hallway. The beam from the lamp jerked on the floor and walls. Our footsteps hammered dully on the wood floor. I didn't like this place, not one bit. We stepped into a larger room with two small cells made of iron bars. A jail!

Suddenly I knew what they were planning. *No!* My legs went stiff. I dug my heels into the floor. But B.J. just drug me along.

When we reached the iron doors, he took off the handcuffs, but I was looking for a way to escape. Iola grabbed my wrist while B.J. untied the handkerchief. Then before I could cry out or break free, Iola gave me a hard push, sending me sprawling on the cell floor. My knees and hands smarted as they scraped the splintered wood. At once I sprang to my feet and rushed for the cell door.

But Iola was quick. She kicked the door and it clanged shut in my face.

"No!" I screamed, my heart hammering. "You can't do this!"

I rattled the bars, hoping to spring the door open. But B.J. held it closed tight as Iola wrapped a chain around the bars. Then they snapped on a large lock.

"Let me out!" I cried. "You're . . . you're . . . you're both common scoundrels!"

Iola leaned close to the bars. I smelled her awful perfume. She said softly, "My dear, I may be many things, scoundrel among them. But one thing I'm not is common."

B.J. nodded. "Iola's a diamond in the rough is what she is."

"Shut up, B.J.," she snarled. Then to me, her voice sickly sweet, she asked, "Now. I'm sure you want to tell me where you hid that notebook?"

Tears welled up in my eyes. My whole body ached. I shook with anger and fear. I'd had enough of Iola Linville and her nasty ways. But I'd never give in to her. Not ever!

"I won't tell you!" I exclaimed. *"Never!"*

Her smile looked wicked in the glow of the lantern. "Well, you have time to think about it," she said. "Plenty of time."

"You can't leave me here," I pleaded. "I'll starve or die of thirst."

"No you won't, girl," B.J. said. He reached through the bars and dropped a canteen and a paper sack onto the floor. "There's water and a couple of sandwiches for you."

Iola added, "You see, dear? I don't intend to hurt you. I just want you to think over your situation. After you've spent a night listening to coyotes howl and a day keeping company with snakes and scorpions, you might be more cooperative."

"Snakes!" B.J. exclaimed. "Iola sugar, did you say there's snakes about?"

Tears rolled from my eyes. I argued, "Tom'll wonder where I've gone off to. He'll look for me."

As soon as I'd said it, I realized the hopelessness of my predicament. Tom himself was in jail. Locked up for something he didn't do.

Iola didn't say another word. She set the kerosene lamp on the floor, turned on her heels, and marched away. B.J. followed like a loyal puppy dog.

Their footsteps faded. Then I heard a door open and slam shut.

I listened carefully until the sound of the car's engine faded. They were gone.

Chapter 12

I sank to the floor of the cell and cried. My whole body ached as I shook with sobs. But my heart ached worse. Why had this happened to me? Why?

My hurt melted away. But in its place came fear. I wiped my tears on my shirt and leaped to my feet. Grabbing the cell bars, I rattled them hard.

"Come back!" I screamed. "I want out! Now!"

Of course, not a sound answered back.

After a time I slid down to the floor and sat hugging my knees in the dusty, dark closeness of the cell.

It struck me then that lately I'd been in some mighty strange and desperate situations. This wasn't even the worst. Fact was, it seemed that since heading west for California weeks ago, I'd been in one dangerous scrape after another. *Why had God let all these things happen to me? Was He testing me? Trying to teach me some lesson? But what lesson? And why pick on a twelve-year-old girl when there were plenty of grown-ups who needed to be taught a lesson?*

Plenty of questions hammered in my brain, but no answers came. I commenced rocking back and forth, trying to make all the doubts go away. My elbow bumped something.

The sack of food.

I plucked it up. The smell of ham drifted from the sack and I felt hungry. Very hungry. Thinking back, I remembered I hadn't eaten since breakfast early that morning. I ripped open the bag and gobbled down the two sandwiches. Then I spied the canteen and took a long drink.

The food and water helped, but I longed for a breath of fresh air. Looking around, I spotted a small, barred window up high on the back wall of the cell. I rushed for it, but my leg struck something hard. *Ow!*

I bent over and felt the thing. A bed. Or at least the iron frame of a bed. I climbed up on it and peered out the window. In the far off clouds I could make out white explosions of lightning like white, jagged teeth.

Stepping down, I settled myself on the cold, hard edge of the bed frame, my face buried in my hands.

Never had I felt so all alone. Not even when I'd been trapped in a dark mine shaft. Then Leo'd been with me. Selfish as it seemed, I wished he were with me now.

My thoughts carried me home to Mama and Daddy. I longed to be with them, safe in their arms. I pictured Mama sitting in a rocking chair humming a favorite hymn. I wanted to be strong like her. I began to sing.

"Amazing grace, how sweet the sound,
That saved a wretch like me.
I once was lost but now I'm found,
Was blind but now I see."

When I paused, I heard it.

A muffled sound.

My heart started beating like mad. I listened. The sound stopped. I looked at the weird, flickering light on the walls and I fretted. Had Iola and B.J. come back? Or could this be someone else? What should I do? Call out or keep still?

Taking a deep breath, I commenced singing again. The words came haltingly to me. "Through many dangers . . . "

The sounds became more distinct. Footsteps? Yes! I heard them in the sheriff's office. Then they echoed down the narrow hallway. My heart leaped to my throat and I choked on the words of the hymn. I balled my hands into fists, waiting.

Then the footsteps stopped.

A shadow appeared in the doorway. The kerosene lamp made it waver along the wall. Then a tall, thin figure emerged.

My whole body quaked. I knew that if I could just get my voice out, I'd scream my fool head off.

"Now why'd you quit singin', missy? That's one of my favorite songs."

Tom!

I jumped up and ran to the bars.

"Tom!" I cried. "Tom, is it really you?"

He reached through the cell door and hugged me tight.

"It's me all right," he replied. He let me loose. I heard the chain rattle against the bars. "I just got out of jail myself. What're *you* in for?" he teased.

"It's that vile Iola Linville and that B.J. They locked me up."

My friend sighed deeply. "I knew trouble was a-brewin'," he said. "And we got ourselves a potful."

"But how'd you get out of jail?" I asked.

"Mr. Dixon. He decided not to press charges. He sprung me just an hour ago. Told me to pack my things and clear out. I got fired. Fired for somethin' I didn't do."

I gasped. "Fired? But for what? And what did they lock you up for?"

"One of the hands on the set found a sack of money—two-hundred-fifty dollars—under a trailer. Iola told Mr. Dixon she'd seen me with it and then commenced to tell him I'd spent time in prison. Can't figure how she happened to know that fact. Anyway, Mr. Dixon figured I stole the money from the studio since they've been coming up short lately."

Oh, dear. It was me. I hung my head in shame.

I reached through the bars and grasped my friend's hand. "Tom, it's all my fault."

"You? I don't—"

I told him about the sack of money. About B.J. hiding it under his bed. How I'd retrieved it and then hid it myself when Iola and B.J. chased me through the moving picture settlement.

"Gracious, missy, none of this's your fault," he said. "I should've never brought you into this snake pit. I'm sorry for that. Powerful sorry."

"But there's something else, Tom," I said.

I felt his eyes on me.

"I told . . . I told Iola you'd been in prison," I confessed. "I didn't mean to. It just slipped out."

His arm came through the bars and patted my back. "Oh, don't you fret over that, missy. Turns out, none of it amounted to a hill of beans. 'Cept losin' my job a'course."

"But how'd you find me way out here?" I asked.

"Your friend from town. Cap McCall. The boy surely keeps unusual hours. I run into him right after I got outta jail. He'd been followin' you and saw those two buzzards grab you right in front of the police station. When he told me what direction they took off in, I figured they might've brought you out this way. We did a day's shootin' near this ol' ghost town. So the movie folks knew about this place."

As Tom fiddled with the lock, I told him everything else that had happened to me—that I'd overheard Iola and B.J. plotting against him and that I'd found Iola's notebook.

"Notebook? What was in it?"

"Just numbers. You know—figures. Lists of figures. I couldn't make heads or tails of it, but Iola sure wanted it back bad. I hid it, but I told Cap to fetch it and give it to Mr. Dixon."

"That could explain a lot of this mystery," Tom said. "If Iola took the missin' money, then that notebook might be a record of her shady dealin's. Seems we stumbled into a bigger mess than I reckoned."

"Yes, and I'm still in a mess," I said. "They locked me

up good, didn't they?"

"So they did," Tom said, giving up on the lock and chain. He chuckled, "Good thing I borrowed one of the studio's trucks. Figured if they wanna believe I'm a thief I might as well live up to my reputation."

Tom picked up the kerosene lamp. "Sit tight, missy," he said, "I'm going outside."

I didn't like getting left alone in the dark, but I figured Tom had a plan worked out. I did what he said. I sat tight and waited. In a few minutes I heard the sound of a vehicle outside the window.

Then I spied shadowy hands reaching between the window bars and looping a rope through them. "Hey, missy," Tom called out, "stand clear of this wall, you hear?"

"OK," I said, moving away. "What're you going to do?"

He didn't answer. Then I heard the truck's engine revving up. At once a loud crack rocked the cell. The bars popped from the window and the wall around it trembled and collapsed. Dust filled the cell and I yanked out my bandanna and covered my face.

After a moment I heard Tom's voice. "You OK, missy?"

"Yes," I choked, fanning the dust.

I saw the yellow glow of the lantern bounce as Tom picked his way through the rubble. I heard him grunt and heard the sound of chunks of adobe being shifted. Then Tom reached for me and led me back through the collapsed wall. It took some doing, but finally we stood together outside in the dark. I breathed in deep the night air. I wondered if Tom had felt like this after getting out of jail. It was so good to be free again.

"I'm glad I took that truck," Tom said, blowing out the lantern. "I ain't sure a horse could've done the job." I heard him chuckle in the pitch dark. "First successful jail break I ever made."

"Me too," I laughed.

Lightning flashed in the distance. Then I heard the low rumble of thunder. It lasted a good long while.

"Missy, we'd best get back to town before the storm hits," Tom suggested. "Looks to be a brutal one."

Before we reached the truck, two bright headlights flashed in my face. My arm flew up to shield my eyes. I froze to the spot.

"Who is it?" I gasped.

But Tom didn't need to answer.

"Well, well, if it isn't the old cowboy and his snoopy little friend."

Iola! Where had she come from? I was sure I'd heard them drive away.

Then B.J.'s voice came at us. "Careful, you two. Me and Iola are armed and dangerous. Aren't we armed and dangerous, Iola?"

"Shut up, B.J."

Dangerous. Yes. Like lightning and thunder. *No,* I thought suddenly. *Those two varmints were far more dangerous than any storm. And they had us good.*

Chapter 13

They stepped close. I made out their forms silhouetted against the glare of the headlights. B.J. held a gun. It looked oddly out of place, like knitting needles would in the hands of Iola.

The vile woman herself stood with her hands on her hips.

"We spotted you, old man, in that truck," Iola declared proudly. "If you thought you could come to the rescue, you were rudely mistaken."

Tom edged in front of me. "Stay back, missy," he whispered.

Skirting around him, I grabbed hold of his arm. I wasn't about to let him do anything foolhardy and get hurt. I blurted, "If this's over that ridiculous notebook, there's no sense in it. I'll give it to you. Then you can be about your business and just leave us alone."

Iola's barked laugh put me in mind of a coyote. She took a step toward us. "I do want that notebook, dear. Make no mistake about that. Too bad I don't believe your good intentions."

Just then lightning flashed low in the clouds. Thunder pounded in the sky like drumbeats. The air hung hot and heavy. I sensed the storm would hit with a fury, and soon. It made me uneasy.

"You have ruined this poor, historic jail," Iola said. "Not to mention our plan. Now we must do something else."

"That was a good sturdy lock and chain too, wasn't it, Iola?" B.J. said.

"Hush up, B.J.," snapped Iola. Then to Tom and me she said, "You two get in the car. The old man in back with B.J. and, dear, you get in front with me."

With the storm coming on, I almost felt grateful for Iola's order. At least in the car we'd be protected.

I took Tom's arm and we shuffled back to the vehicle. B.J. slammed the door after Tom, and I slid in the front seat. We left behind the studio truck Tom had taken. Soon Iola headed the car down a rutted dirt road. I feared this direction would lead us even farther away from Flintrock.

After a moment I rustled up the nerve to speak. "Just what are your intentions?" I asked Iola.

She glared at me. The green lights from the dashboard made her look sick. "Strictly honorable," she answered, then exploded with laughter.

Her strange behavior upset me. It put me in mind of a crazed person.

"What are our intentions, sugar?" B.J. asked her. "What're you aiming to do with these folks?"

"That's for me to know and for them to find out, B.J.," Iola replied. "And quit calling me 'sugar'!"

The lightning flashes came quicker now, giving me glimpses of faraway hills. Thunder pounded like round after round of cannon fire.

"Keep your eyes open, B.J.," she commanded.

"Uh, right, sug—Iola," B.J. said. "Uh, Iola?"

"What?" the woman answered irritably.

"What exactly am I supposed to keep my eyes open for?"

"For a place to dump these two!" Iola cried. "Do I have to spell out *every*thing?"

Her words "dump these two" sent a chill through me. Crazed or not, this woman had no shred of common decency or kindness in her. That much I knew to be true.

"Look!" B.J. exclaimed. "Over there!"

"Where?"

He tapped his pistol against the window glass as if pointing. "There. On the left. Looks like a little bitty hill."

"Well, let's go take a look," Iola said.

With that, she swung the car to the left, cutting away from the rough road and bouncing over rocky ground. Tall grass brushed against the sides of the car. The headlights flared up over the terrain, revealing a large herd of cattle grazing in the distance. Then the lights touched a hulking object nearby.

Dread filled me. What would come of all this? Would I ever be back with Mama and Daddy? Or back on Will Rogers' ranch? I longed for home, where danger didn't lurk every which way.

As we got closer, I made out the object in the pasture. Just an old car. Its tires and doors missing, the hulk reminded me of a dead cow's bones.

Iola stomped on the brake pedal, and we stopped close to the old wreck.

"All right, dears, get out," she commanded. "And don't you forget. B.J. still has his gun."

I didn't need to be reminded of that fact. Though B.J. didn't scare me much, I didn't like the way he waved that gun around. Like he considered it a toy. Besides, I still feared Tom might try something desperate and get himself hurt.

But my friend came along silently as I headed for the abandoned car. Lightning continued to split the black clouds. The air felt different now—crackly and crisp, the heaviness gone. I almost expected to see sparks shoot up from the grass when the lightning flashed. Tom and I hesitated at the wreck. The crazed Iola, B.J. and his gun, the thunder and lightning. This night seemed full of menace.

"Climb in, dears," Iola said almost cheerfully. "Hurry now."

B.J. chimed in. "That's right. Me and Iola don't want to get caught in this storm. Do we, Iola?"

I saw that the old car had a front seat, a steering wheel, and not much else. One of the doors lay beside it in the grass.

"I said *get in!*" Iola yelled.

I held tight to Tom and pulled him into the wreck. The

rotten seat cover creaked and split as we settled ourselves.

"B.J., the handcuffs," Iola instructed.

Handing his gun to Iola, he leaned into the car. He grabbed my wrist and snapped on the handcuff. Then pulling my arm forward, he looped the loose end of the handcuff through the steering wheel and snapped it on Tom's wrist. He backed away.

I yanked my arm. The handcuffs held tight. Tom yanked hard himself. No luck.

"Don't you get wet now," Iola called out as she and B.J. disappeared into the beam of the headlights. "And, dear, you think long and hard about giving back what rightfully belongs to me. You understand? The notebook?"

"Iola Linville, you come back here and set us free," Tom yelled, still jerking on the handcuffs.

But she didn't answer. I heard two doors slam. In a moment the car backed away. The sound of the engine and the lights quickly faded.

Tom and I were stranded in the wilderness.

Chapter 14

I huddled close to Tom as thunder boomed over us. He'd stopped jerking the handcuffs. He sat slumped and silent, like a worn out old man.

"I'm sorry I got you into this fix," I said, feeling old and worn out myself.

"We're in this fix together," he replied in a tired voice. "And it ain't none of it your doin'."

"But what're we going to do?"

Tom didn't answer for a spell, as if thinking over our predicament. "Don't rightly know, missy," he admitted.

I looked through the broken out windshield. When the lightning flashed, I noticed the cows had huddled together. They made low noises that sounded like groaning.

"Those cows seem kind of skittish," I said.

"Yep," Tom agreed, "sometimes a storm can spook a herd pretty bad. Even make 'em stampede."

Stampede? I put that thought right out of my mind. It seemed safer to consider the villainous Iola Linville than a herd of runaway cattle.

I said, "Do you think Iola will come back for us?"

"She will if she wants that blamed notebook," Tom

answered, some spunk returning to his voice. "And don't you give it to her neither. If she wants it that bad, it must incriminate her somethin' awful."

I considered for a moment what would be worse—Iola coming back and threatening us some more, or her leaving us stranded out here for good. My mind couldn't sort it out. Like I'd asked Iola, I wanted to ask God, *Just what are Your intentions, Lord?*

As Tom jiggled the handcuffs again, I offered up a silent prayer. *Lord, I do appreciate Your sending Tom to rescue me from that jail cell. I really do. You've been pretty good about delivering me from these scrapes. But I'm getting perplexed. I doubt You want to keep throwing calamity at me. So why are all these things happening?*

Tom's sighing put an end to my confused prayer. He settled back in the car's creaky seat and said, "Missy, none of this has turned out the way I reckoned it would. This movie business—it's pure trouble, more trouble than a band of outlaws at a bankers meeting. And I should've seen it comin', but I got my mind too set on keepin' that blamed job."

I nestled close, wanting to comfort him. "Don't worry, Tom," I said. Then a perfectly wonderful idea struck me. "I know! When we get back home, let's go see Will Rogers. He's a fine man, a regular person just like you and me. I'll bet he'd give you a job in *his* moving pictures."

"It's a good thought, missy," Tom replied. "But I've pretty much had all the movie business I can stomach. I've been thinkin' 'bout going back to Missouri. See if maybe I could search out my wife and daughter. They might want nothin' to do with me, but I've kinda got a hankerin' to see 'em. 'Specially since I ain't seen them in forty-three years."

"Oh, Tom, that'd be a real good thing," I said. "But I'd miss you like the dickens."

A narrow vein of lightning lit up the sky. For an instant I saw clear as day the rusted, beaten-up hood of the car, the cattle in front of us, and the wide pasture land.

Something strange happened right before my eyes. As the lightning flashed again, the horns of the cattle commenced to glowing blue.

"What's *that?*" I cried, pointing at the herd.

Tom sat up and leaned over the steering wheel.

"Ain't seen that in quite a spell," he told me. "St. Elmo's fire. Used to occur pretty often on cattle drives. Quite a sight, ain't it?"

"Yes," I admitted, my eyes fixed on the scene. "But kind of spooky."

The glowing lasted for a time, then large wet drops of rain began splattering down through the open windshield. Once the rain started, the cows' horns looked regular again.

"We're gonna get mighty wet," Tom observed.

I shivered from the rain, the dark, and the emptiness. "I just wish we could get out of here," I said.

A lightning bolt flashed—the long, jagged line shooting from high in the clouds to the ground right near the wreck. Then following it—

CCCRRRRAAAAAAAAAAAACCCKKKKKK!

The ear-splitting thunder made me jump in the seat.

"Whoa!" I yelled, my heart beating like mad.

"Hang on there, girl," Tom said, though I could tell from his voice he'd been shaken too.

The cattle's mooing grew louder. Although I couldn't see them clearly, I sensed their nervousness. I heard them begin to move.

"I don't like the looks of that herd," Tom said. I felt his body tense. He leaned forward, trying to see through the darkness and the rain.

With the next flash of lightning came another thundering sound. This time, though, it didn't come from the clouds. It rose up from the pasture.

Hoofbeats! The herd was stampeding!

I gripped Tom's arm tight. Lightning lit up the sky. Then I saw the cattle hadn't headed our way but off in another direction. Thank goodness. I relaxed.

The sky lit up again, and again.

I pressed back in the seat, trying to get out of the rain, but the water still drenched me.

I heard Tom gasp. "Oh, no."

Leaning forward, I peered into the darkness, this time ignoring the freezing rain pelting my face. I couldn't make out a thing. But I heard something. The sound of cattle's hooves pounding the earth. The noise grew louder and louder. With the next flash of lightning I saw the herd charging right toward the rust-eaten car.

"Tom," I cried, *"they're gonna trample us!"*

Chapter 15

A fierce roar rose up as the cattle's hooves hammered the ground. In the dark, the noise and the charging black mass reminded me of a runaway train.

"We gotta get out, gotta run for it!" Tom shouted.

"No! Oh, no!" I cried back. I wanted to shrink down to the ground. To make myself tiny enough to hide in a hole until the danger had passed.

"If they trample the car, we're done for!" cried Tom. He kicked the dashboard and his boot shot on through, proving his point.

"Oh no!" I exclaimed again, understanding at that moment that the rusted-out hulk offered no protection whatsoever.

I yanked hard on the handcuff, hoping it would snap apart, but it held my wrist tight. Meanwhile the pounding of the hooves grew louder. With each flash of lightning I spied the herd coming closer and closer.

In my fear I lashed out. I jerked, trying to free myself, until pain shot through my arm. Then I kicked the floorboard, the dashboard, anything I could reach.

My desperate fit must've given Tom an idea.

"Hey, that-a-girl!" he encouraged. "Stomp at the steer-

ing column. Maybe it'll break free."

Together we kicked that old car till my feet burned.

Then it happened! The steering wheel and the column jerked loose.

"Quick, missy, run!" Tom yelled.

We leaped from the vehicle, dragging the steering wheel and column between us. I ran as fast as I could. Still, Tom had to drag me along. All at once I could smell the heavy odor of wet animals breathing hard, bearing down on us. I glanced back. Lightning flashed and my heart leaped in my chest. Cattle! Hundreds of heads of them. Right on our heels!

We kept running. My legs felt on fire and my arm throbbed something fierce. Still, we kept running.

Tom gasped, "Faster, missy, faster!"

At that moment I hurt so bad I wanted to collapse on the ground. To just let those cows stomp right over me. I didn't stop, though. I couldn't. Tom kept pulling me along.

Suddenly my arm jerked. The ground fell out from under me and I pitched forward.

I tumbled after Tom down a long black slope. For a moment I hurtled through the air. Then my body crashed to the earth, hard. I rolled across the rough ground. Each rock that I hit, each twist of my arm brought a sharp stab of pain. I felt like my arm was being wrenched right off. Then, just as I thought I would surely die, we stopped.

For a time, I just lay still, my whole body aching. My throat burned as I gasped for air. My fingers reached into a cool, muddy ooze. My face rested in shallow, dirty water which lapped into my mouth.

I kept lying there, waiting. Waiting for those cows to trample me.

But it didn't happen. Instead, the freight train roar of the hooves grew fainter. The rain stopped pounding. Soon I heard nothing at all.

"Tom," I gasped, "wh—what happened?"

He didn't answer. At first I panicked, fearing the fall had knocked him out. Then I felt him fumbling in the dark, as if taking stock of himself, making sure he still had all his parts.

"Missy, you all right?" he croaked.

"I—I think so," I groaned. I tested my arms, my legs, to see if they still worked. It hurt to move, but I didn't think anything was broken.

Tom sat up slowly beside me. I pushed up too, out of the muddy water. The steering wheel still hung between us, but the column must've broken off somewhere.

"I never had a particular fondness for the cow," Tom remarked wearily. He stood up slowly and helped me to my feet. "And I haven't changed that view none."

As I reached up to brush strands of dirty, wet hair out of my face, my handcuff popped open and dropped loose. The steering wheel thudded to the ground. I held up my freed wrist, marveling at it. I rubbed it to ease the soreness. Then reaching over, I took hold of Tom's wrist. My fingers found a small button on the handcuff and I pressed it. The handcuff snapped open and dropped to the ground.

"They weren't real handcuffs," I said, amazed. "Nothing but a moving picture prop!"

For a moment we stared in the dark at each other. I couldn't see Tom's face, but I heard him. He started chuckling. Then I started in too. We'd been so close to being trampled to death by cattle, but now all we could do was laugh.

Later, trudging through the dark in what we hoped to be the direction of Flintrock, I still had to laugh. The cattle stampede, the fake handcuffs. Who'd ever believe such a tale?

* * *

Tom led the way, using the red flames of the rising sun as his compass. As the sky brightened, I could see his face. I noticed two wide, nasty scratches along his jaw.

"Are you OK?" I cried, reaching up to touch his injuries.

He winced slightly. "Just tuckered out is all. You got plenty of scrapes on you too. Fact is, you got yourself scrapes on top of scrapes," he said. I remembered getting blown up in the explosion. It seemed like a hundred years ago.

"Mostly I'm just tired too," I admitted. "But I'm not stopping. Not till we get to town and report Iola to the police."

"Let's just get ourselves back to town first. Then we can decide what to do about her."

As the sun kept rising in the sky, I was stunned by the

landscape. No trace remained of last night's storm. Not even an occasional pool of rainwater. Everything looked dry, like the earth had sucked up every drop. Only my wet, dirty clothes and my scratches and bruises testified that the dangers we'd faced had been real.

"How much farther?" I asked Tom, my weariness taking over.

He eyed me. Draping his own bruised arm around my shoulder, he said, "Another five miles or so I'd guess. Missy, do you want to rest a spell before we go on?"

"No," I insisted. "Let's keep going."

A long time passed. Then, finally, I caught sight of the trucks, trailers, and moving picture sets.

"There it is!" I cried weakly.

We trudged into the camp to find no one about except a lone guard.

"Where's everyone gone?" Tom asked the man.

The guard eyed us suspiciously. No doubt we looked like a sorry pair. Finally, he seemed to recognize Tom and he answered, "They're all out at the canyon, east o' here."

"Oh, that's right," Tom said, slapping his hand against his leg. "I plumb forgot. They're shootin' that big train scene this mornin'."

"Let's go tell Mr. Dixon what happened," I said.

Tom pulled me aside. "Missy, Walt Dixon's been worried sick for weeks about this train scene. He won't cotton to seein' either of us out there. What say I take you back to the hotel so you can get some shut-eye. Then I'll head out to the canyon and try and get a word with Mr. Dixon. I'll tell him what you told me—about the sack of money and the notebook. And I can tell him what I saw at the train station yesterday mornin'. When I came to pick you up."

"What did you see?"

"Iola. She'd come in to pick up the payroll. She took a big wad of foldin' money outta the payroll bag and stuffed it into her purse."

"That's it, Tom! She's been stealing the money. I want to go with—"

"Your mama'd want you to listen to me," he cautioned.

I smiled wearily at him and nodded. He was right. Iola or no Iola, at that moment what I needed was sleep.

Tom convinced the guard to let him borrow a studio car, and he drove me the last mile back to town.

Once inside the hotel, I got another room key from the desk clerk. I crept up the stairs, barely able to keep my eyes open and my legs moving. I staggered into my room and collapsed on the bed. I didn't even bother to take off my damp, dirty clothes.

Just when I'd nearly drifted off to sleep, voices in the hall startled me awake. Familiar voices. I dragged myself up and went to the door to listen.

I heard B.J. say, "Iola, sugar, I just seen him. *I seen him!*" He spoke loud and quick, like an excited child.

"You saw who?" Iola demanded.

"That old man. Tom whatshisname. The one we—you know—"

"*Saw* him?" came Iola's voice, amazed. "Saw him where?"

"From my window," replied B.J. "Driving by in a studio car."

"You must be mistaken," Iola countered, her voice seething with anger.

"No, sugar. I saw him plain as day."

"Call me 'sugar' again, and I'll handcuff you to an abandoned car," Iola warned.

"I bet he's on his way to find Dixon and tell him what we did," B.J. said. "We'll be in a heap of trouble then."

"No, we won't," Iola snapped, "because we won't let him get to Walt. We'll fix him good this time."

I was too tired to think straight, too tired to care what might happen to me. All I heard was more plotting against Tom. My anger rose up, giving me a burst of energy. I'd had it with these two. I wouldn't let them do one more thing to bring harm to my friend. I'd put a halt to their schemes once and for all. They'd be plenty sorry they ever met up with Jessie Land.

I flung open the door and stormed out into the hall.

Chapter 16

Iola's face went white and her eyes widened at the sight of me. Squinting, B.J. scratched his head like he couldn't believe what he saw.

I shouted at them, "You varmints leave Tom be. You nearly got us killed already. And I'm telling Mr. Dixon and the police all about it. You'll be plenty sorry!"

Iola snarled, "My dear, you just made a grave mistake. Now you'll be the sorry one."

I caught the dangerous gleam in her eyes. She motioned for B.J. and the two of them stepped closer. But I didn't wait around to get grabbed. I dashed for the stairs, flying down them two and three steps at a time.

"After her, you fool!" Iola yelled.

Footsteps hammered behind me. "Come here, girl!" B.J. called.

I hit the lobby floor and raced for the front door. Then I plunged outside. I wanted to get to the police station. But I couldn't remember which way to go. My mind had gone blank.

I darted left and ran half way down the hot street. Then I stopped and looked back. Surely B.J. and Iola wouldn't chase me in broad daylight. A few folks milled about. I spied some kids playing marbles in the shade of an alley, a pesky puppy dog clambering over them. A couple of women came out of a store, looking forlorn and talking quietly to one another. Some old men sweated on a wooden bench in front of the post office. None of them seemed interested in me.

I watched as B.J. and Iola came out of the hotel. They spotted me right away and pointed in my direction. The kids playing marbles looked up at them. I recognized the tall red-headed boy from the outskirts of the moving picture camp and the little boy with the tin pot on his head. I didn't see Cap McCall.

To my surprise Iola and B.J. didn't take out after me. Instead, Iola hurried over and talked to the town kids. She pointed at me and all the kids turned and looked.

Suddenly, the redhead jumped up.

"C'mon guys!" he yelled.

The other kids hopped up too. They began fanning out and moving in my direction. One of them shouted: *"Let's get her!"*

What! I couldn't believe it. Why would they come after me? I didn't wait to find out. I took off down the street, hopping over a pile of feed sacks and dodging a woman with a small child in tow. I was tired of running. Tired of Iola Linville and her sneaky ways. But I'd acted the fool for confronting her and B.J. outside my room. Now I had no choice but to keep running.

I dashed down an alley, the kids calling out behind me. Spying an old Ford pickup truck parked at the other end, I sprinted for it then hid behind its front tire. I heard the kids halt on the other side of the truck.

"Where'd she go?"

"Dunno. Didja see 'er, Red?'

"Naw. But we'll git her awright."

The kids stood just a few feet away—so close! My heart pounded so loud I feared it would give me away.

"What'd that movie lady say about her, Red?"

"She said the girl's gotten herself in a real pickle. Stole a lotta money from the director fella an' then tried to tell 'im us kids from town took it. Now we're all kicked off the set 'cause o' her."

"The no good liar!"

All lies!

Iola had poisoned their minds against me! If I showed myself now, they'd jump me, maybe beat me up. Or worse—turn me over to Iola. I had to get away. I huddled behind the pickup trying to think up a plan. Going back through town would be dangerous. Some kid would spot me before I even got near the police station. If only I could get to the canyon and find Tom. Then I'd be safe.

"C'mon, you guys," I heard Red say. "Let's spread out."

I had no choice. I'd have to run again.

A few feet away, out in the street, I spied two bare-chested men leaning against an old wooden handcart loaded with white bags. I waited for my chance. Then I took a deep breath, balled my hands into fists, and lit out.

"Hey! There she goes!" some kid yelled.

I flew toward the men with their cart. Hopping up on it, I tromped across the bags. White powder puffed up around me. Flour.

One of the men grabbed for me, but I leaped past him, hitting the ground hard.

"Hey you, kid!" the man yelled. I turned right and scrambled down another street. Trying not to call attention to myself, I jumped onto the sidewalk and marched briskly past some boarded-up windows. Words scrawled on the wood read, *Closed for Business* and *Flat Busted* and *We Give Up*.

It was a hard life in Flintrock, Arizona for merchants, folks out of work, and young girls being chased by crazed children.

I peeked around a corner. No sign of the town kids. No Iola or B.J. Had I escaped them at last? Leaning against the wooden building, I rested a moment. With my eyes shut, I took deep breaths, trying to think. Where's that plan, Jessie? I knew I had to get to the canyon, but I had no idea where it was. If only someone, someone kindly, would direct me.

Finally, I pushed away from the building and walked toward a house. A shack made of tin really. In the yard two ragged children played, scooting small wooden boxes about in the dirt. A woman at the side of the house pinned clothes on a line. She looked nice enough. I headed for her.

I hadn't taken five steps when I heard it. The stomp of feet running, chasing. The cries of "This way!" and "Hey, over there!"

Then they appeared.

A whole pack of kids ran right for me! Angry kids set on revenge for the wrong they thought I'd done them. Part of me wanted to stay, to explain. I didn't want those kids to hate me. But I didn't want them to catch me either. Running and yelling like that, they didn't seem in a mind to listen to the truth.

I took off. As fast as I could, I raced behind the tin shack, leaped over a falling down fence, and dashed across a porch. A dog commenced to howling and I ran faster.

Down another alley I sped, looking for a place to hide.

I heard yelling not far behind me.

The alley turned left. I shot that way. On the right I spotted a door with a flap of cardboard covering the bottom half. Maybe the door was broken. Maybe I could hide in there. *Please, God,* I prayed.

I swallowed and dived headlong for the cardboard. It gave way and I scrambled through on my hands and knees into a dark, musty-smelling room. Quickly, I propped the cardboard back over the opening.

My head and heart pounding, I leaned against the door and listened. Footsteps, running, and cries of the kids came from the alley. The pack had swept past my hiding place.

Thank You, God.

I caught my breath and backed slowly away from the door. I glanced around. Light streamed in through gaps in the boarded-up front window. I saw dusty, empty shelves and some broken-down tables along the walls.

I heard scurrying in the dark corners of the room. Mice? Rats? I decided not to investigate and headed for the front window to peek outside.

Stepping carefully over a few boxes and such, I made my way through the building. Then I heard something. A sound like whispering came from the corner, near the window. I shook my head. *No, Jessie,* I told myself, *it's only your imagination.* I kept creeping forward.

Then the sound came again. Yes. Whispering. I was sure of it!

I stopped dead still, holding my breath. Who could it be? I knew no town kids had followed me in here.

Swallowing hard, I got up my courage. I tiptoed toward a pile of broken, wooden crates stacked in the corner. The sound had come from over there.

When I got close, I hesitated. I peeked around the crates, hoping to see but not be seen.

A child's gasp greeted me. There in the dim light I saw them. A woman about Mama's age and four small children, one of them stark naked. They stared up at me with wide eyes. None of them spoke. At their bare feet I noticed an overturned tin can. Beans spilled from it onto the dirty floor. They huddled together on a ragged looking mat. It came to me at once that these pitiful folks lived in this place.

I tried to smile at them so they wouldn't fear me. But they only stared back, their eyes blank. I felt bad, like I'd barged in where I had no business being. I edged away.

At the front window, I turned from the poor family and

peered out. I spotted a clump of kids in front of the boarded-up building. The red-haired boy held a stick and beat at the dust in the street. I could tell he was angry. No doubt he'd sooner be whacking me. After a while, the group headed up the street.

I glanced back at the corner. The family still huddled there, unmoving and silent. Waiting for me to leave. I stayed at the window a good long time, waiting myself, watching for a chance to escape.

Across the street I spied a garage. In front of it sat a black car, one of those big old Packards like my aunt in Liberal, Kansas drove. Just inside the door of the garage, a man in grimy coveralls and a red baseball cap bent over a bench, busy at work. Above the door I could make out the words of a faded sign.

Honest work on your vehicle at low rates

Could I trust that man? I'd have to have someone's help if I hoped to get to the canyon and find Tom. I gazed at the sign again. If you couldn't trust a garage mechanic who told you he did honest work cheap, who could you trust?

I decided to give him a try.

I glanced one last time at the corner. The family remained frozen, like five statues. My heart ached for them. But I knew I couldn't help them, not at the moment leastwise.

I undid the latch and eased the door open. It creaked

something fierce.

Creeping outside, I shut the door behind me and looked in both directions. Not a soul in sight.

I slowly stepped out into the burning street, my eyes searching this way and that for the pack of kids. Still no sign of them.

Then, fast as I could, I crossed over and crouched low next to the Packard. Though the car hid me from the garage, I realized any kid who happened by could see me plain as day.

OK, Jessie, now what do you do?

I heard men talking inside the garage.

"Joe, I'm headin' out to the canyon now," a deep voice said.

The canyon!

"OK," replied another man. "I'll wait till ya get back 'fore I take lunch."

"Sure you don't want to come along?" the deep voice asked. "That train scene'll be some sight. Won't hurt to close up for an hour or so."

The man with the deep voice planned to go watch the train scene! Would he agree to take me along?

"Naw," the other man said. "I gotta fix this oil leak. But wouldja get me some coffee 'fore ya go?"

"Sure thing."

Then I saw the man in the red baseball cap come out of the garage and head for the café next door. My chance! But how could I convince him to take me along, a kid he'd never laid eyes on before? I could say some mean kids from his miserable town were chasing me. Or that an evil woman named Iola wanted my hide. Probably he wouldn't appreciate my calling his town "miserable." And somehow these reasons didn't seem very good.

Then, as I fretted and watched for the man to return, I spotted the gang of kids in the street only a block away. The redhead strutted along in front and the whole group headed toward me.

No! Not again, I groaned. I buried my face in my hands. I didn't want to run another step.

What now, God? Does this mean I should just give up?

Chapter 17

I heard a footstep nearby and raised my head.

There, at the front of the Packard, between me and the town kids, stood Cap McCall.

Maybe I wouldn't have to give up after all. Maybe this truly was my chance!

Frowning, Cap said, "I see ya got away from those characters."

Behind him, the kids in the street kept moving closer.

"Not quite," I whispered. "Please, help me."

My plea set him into action. He bolted forward, opened the back door of the Packard, and gave me a shove.

"Get down on the floor," he ordered.

I did just like he said. I curled up in a tight, little ball on the floor of the car. A thin, brown blanket covered the rear seat, and Cap yanked it off and threw it over me. It felt scratchy and smelled like a wet dog, but I didn't care. Even in that stuffy, cramped space, I breathed easier. Cap McCall, at least, would help me.

I heard a kid shout and Cap answered back. Then the sound of footsteps came from the street. The driver's door opened. Someone climbed in the car. The door slammed shut.

"C'mon, Cap," the man with the deep voice called out. "You goin' or not?"

"Yeah, I'm comin', Pop," Cap answered.

Pop? The mechanic was Cap's father! I heard the passenger door open and close.

"What'd Red and them kids want?" Cap's father asked.

"They're just clownin' around," Cap replied.

"Well, they didn't look like they was clownin'. Red's just plain mean. You stay clear a him, you hear?"

"Sure, Pop."

The engine started up and we set out. I grinned to myself. Soon, very soon, I'd be at the canyon! And be with Tom. I knew then everything would work out fine.

The car rocked along. I wanted to pull the scratchy cover off my face and breathe fresh air. But would Cap's father be mad if he saw me? I didn't know, but I sure didn't want to get Cap in trouble, so I stayed put.

I could just barely hear Cap and his father speaking over the hum of the engine. I picked up the words "Babe" and "home run," so I figured them to be talking about baseball. After a while, though, their words ran together, sounding something like the buzzes of flies against a screen door. My mind drifted and my eyes grew heavy. I felt downright weary. In a few minutes I fell asleep.

I dreamed I was back in town. A whole slew of people chased me. I saw Red and the faces of those poor, hungry children in that boarded-up building.

The car jolted and I woke up, glad for the dream to end.

Suddenly the car stopped. I heard the driver's door open and slam shut. I lay still for a while, waiting for Cap to give me a signal. Then, just when I determined to peek out, the blanket yanked off and I looked straight into Cap's face.

He leaned over the front seat, staring at me.

Finally I said, "I appreciate your hiding me from those kids."

He balled up the blanket and threw it onto the back seat. "What was they chasin' you for anyway?" he asked.

"They thought I stole something and blamed them for it," I said, edging up on the seat. "That it was my fault they got kicked off the moving picture set."

"You ain't a thief, are you?" he asked.

"Of course not!" I protested. "It was that vile Iola Linville. She lied about me and stirred up those kids."

"If I hadn't seen her and that big fella grab you last night, I oughta be mad. You shouldn't go about callin' my cousin 'vile.' "

I gaped at him. "Your *cousin?*"

"Pop's cousin really. She's from Flintrock, born and raised here. Folks 'round here think a lot of her ownin' to the fact that she talked those movie folks into shootin' their picture out here. Supposed to lift Flintrock clear outta the Depression. The town even gave 'em the old train to use in the movie."

"Well, like it or not, your pop's cousin's involved in something shady," I said. "And I can prove it."

"Ya mean with that notebook?" Cap asked.

I gazed at the boy, hopeful I'd been right to trust him. "That's part of it. Did you do like I said?"

Cap started to smile. Then his face paled. At once he commenced to feeling his pockets.

"What?" I gasped. "What'd you do with it?"

He didn't meet my gaze. "I—I got it from under your mattress."

"And?"

His eyes darted this way and that. He wouldn't look straight at me. "Well, I ain't sure. I stuck it in my pocket last night, but what with the commotion of you gettin' grabbed and such . . . And then Pop took me ridin' around in Mr. Dixon's car to check it out. I don't know. I—I guess I just plumb forgot about it. And now, well, I can't seem to . . ." The boy's voice trailed off.

"So now it's lost is what you're saying," I said, sick at heart.

Looking down, he mumbled, "I guess so."

I wanted to be angry with him. Even to yell at him. The notebook! Tom himself had said it must contain proof of Iola's wrongdoing. And now Cap had lost it. But I couldn't find it in me to be mad.

Reaching up, I touched the boy's shoulder. "Well, maybe it'll turn up," I said hopefully. "I do thank you for trying. And thanks for telling Tom about Iola and B.J. kidnapping me last night. Tom came to my rescue, but we nearly got ourselves killed. Thanks to Iola."

Cap glanced out the window. He shrugged and said, "Don't surprise me none. I never much cared for her myself. She's downright sneaky." He looked at me. "So how *did* you escape from them?" he asked. He seemed eager to get off the subject of the notebook.

"It's quite a tale, but I'll have to tell you later, OK?"

He nodded. I peeked out the car window. Just a few feet away a crowd of people stood about. They talked and pointed and acted like children lined up to ride a roller coaster. Off to the right I spotted a big black locomotive with five cars hooked to it. The tracks stretched straight ahead and large white clouds of steam poured from the engine's smokestack. I wondered what made this train scene so all-fired exciting.

"I've got to find Tom," I said. "Iola's plotting against him and he may be in danger. Will you help me?"

Cap nodded right off. He made up his mind quick. I liked that about him.

I opened the door and climbed out of the car.

I looked around for Tom and Mr. Dixon but couldn't spot either one of them. I did spy Winnie, though. She wore her cowgirl outfit and fake hair and stood twirling a parasol close to the back of the train. Then I watched her walk around the rear of the caboose and disappear.

A voice crackling through a megaphone called out, "Now listen up, folks! To watch the end of the train scene, take the canyon road south. And be sure and stay behind the roped-off area. We'll get underway in just a few minutes."

I scanned the crowd, still searching for Tom. Where was he?

Cap nudged me. “Uh oh, Jessie, it’s her.”

I looked where he pointed. Through the crowd I caught sight of Iola. The crowd had thinned out as folks hurried to their cars. In a moment the villain would spot me.

An idea popped into my head. I told Cap, “I’m going to ask Winnie if she’s seen Tom. But I don’t want Iola to see me.”

His eyes brightened. “I’ll keep ’er busy,” he piped up. He dashed off.

I ducked behind the Packard and watched Cap run up to Iola and commence talking to her. She didn’t look any too pleased to see him. I sure felt grateful for him. Grateful for any friend in these parts. I weaved through the crowd, wedging myself between one person after another so Iola wouldn’t notice me. I glanced back at Cap and Iola. He still had her occupied.

Then, unexpectedly, I bumped into someone. I turned around and looked up. Right into the smiling face of B.J. Seeds.

“Well, hello, girl,” he said, grasping my arm. “We got you now. Bet you thought you got away from us, didn’t you? Now we’ve just gotta find that old man.”

I started to cry out, but B.J.’s other hand clamped over my mouth. People milled around us, completely ignoring the fact that a large man held a young girl captive. What was the matter with them? I struggled, but it was useless.

“Let’s me and you go see Iola,” B.J. said pleasantly. “She’ll be happy to see you, don’t you think?”

I’d had enough of Iola Linville to last me a lifetime. I

would not go willingly.

As B.J. started to steer me toward her, I chomped down on his hand as hard as I could. I lashed out with the heel of my shoe, striking his shin hard.

"Yee-oowwww!" he cried out, jumping in pain. For an instant he relaxed his grip on me. I scrambled away. I heard him yell, *"Hey, Iola!"*

Then I broke into a clearing and stood all alone. Ahead lay the train. I sprinted for it. I ducked under the heavy coupling that joined two cars and dashed toward the back of the train.

I found Winnie sitting on the bottom step of the caboose. Shading her face with a lacy green parasol, she fanned herself with a matching lacy green fan. When she saw me, she stopped dead still, her eyes wide.

"You!" she cried, standing up. "I thought we'd seen the last of you.'

"Please, Winnie, have you seen Tom?" I asked, trying to be nice. "Or Mr. Dixon?"

"Maybe I have and maybe I haven't," she sassed. "What business is that of yours? Just go away."

So much for being nice.

I'd run plumb out of patience with these moving picture folks. I grabbed Winnie by the arm and gave her a little shake.

"Tell me where they are," I demanded.

A stubborn look crossed her pudgy face. She yanked hard, breaking my hold on her. Then she backed up the steps of the caboose.

"You stay away from me!" she cried, shaking her fake golden locks. "I don't have to tell you anything. *Go away!*"

Fearing B.J. would appear any moment, I mustered up all the threat I could. I threw a look of stubborn determination right back at her and followed her up the steps.

"I've got no time to waste on you," I said, grabbing her parasol and leaning real close. "You'd best tell me now. Where's Tom and Mr. Dixon?"

"You get away!" she shouted. She started slapping at my face with her fan and backed the rest of the way up the steps until she stood at the door of the caboose. *"Stay away!* Stay away from me!"

Her voice sounded high and scared. Like I was some kind of wild animal she had to escape from. I feared she was becoming completely crazed. But mostly I feared her fool yelling would give me away.

I sprang toward her. In that instant, as she jerked back, I glimpsed B.J. steadily picking his way toward the train.

In only seconds he'd catch me all over again!

Chapter 18

Winnie let go a scream. But I shot forward, clamping my hand over her mouth and managing to muffle most of it. She scooted backward through the opened door of the caboose. I followed her in.

"Winnie, take it easy," I said in a soft voice, intent on calming her. "I'm not out to harm you, so there's no reason to yell out."

Inside, the caboose had been stripped of its furnishings. Dust balls and a few scraps of paper spun on the floor as a hot breeze drifted in. A large, battered, wooden crate lay on its side near the back of the car. The door at the other end had been secured with a large padlock.

"Winnie, Winnie," I whispered, "hush up now."

Her blue eyes wide with fear, she kept swatting at me with her fan as she backed herself into the corner behind the crate. I knew I'd have to do something to calm her down or the girl might go plumb crazy.

"Winnie, please, it's all right," I crooned.

I didn't know what else to do, so I just reached out and put my arms around her, hugging her tight. I felt her whole body relax. Then she huddled, silent but shaking in the corner. At that moment I felt so sorry for Winnie

Collins that my heart ached. She didn't seem mean and obnoxious anymore, just plain sad and scared. Like any other kid hit by hard times and trouble. Maybe she'd been right. Maybe it wasn't so easy being a child star.

I kept my hold on Winnie for the longest time. All the while I heard cars pulling away outside. Soon the quiet outside matched the quiet inside the caboose. Finally, I let loose of her and pulled back. I thought now she might come to like me a little, even see that I wasn't a ragamuffin after all.

"Poo!" she said. "How long's it been since you had a bath?"

I looked at my hands and tried wiping them on my filthy overalls. Winnie had me there. I sorely needed a good scrubbing.

"Any decent person would use soap and water," the actress nagged.

I got ready to defend myself. After all, not even Winnie Collins would stay clean if she'd been through my adventures. But just then Cap exploded through the door of the caboose, his floppy cloth cap flying off.

"There you are!" he cried. "I've been lookin' for you all over."

Suddenly the train jerked to a start.

The motion threw me against Winnie. She fell back on the floor. BANG! went the door. I steadied myself, then got up and offered Winnie my hand. Her gold curls were turned sideways. I reached down to straighten her wig. She slapped my hand away and adjusted it herself.

"Jessie, we've gotta—" Cap yelled. *"Oh, no!* This dad-blasted door!"

"Just a minute," I told him as I helped Winnie to her feet. When I looked back at Cap, he was busy yanking on the door and kicking it with his dirty bare feet.

He turned and started to say something when he caught sight of who stood next to me. "Hey, that's Winnie Collins."

Winnie peeked around me to get a look at him.

"Another ragamuffin with a bad haircut," she grumbled. She smoothed her costume and fanned her face. Then she shoved her way past me and stepped to the window. "We're—we're—we're *moving!"* she gasped.

I went over to stand beside her and looked out. "They must be shooting the train scene everybody's been talking about."

"Hey, you two, quit jabberin'!" Cap yelled, still yanking at the caboose door. "I tell ya we gotta git outta here!"

The train rumbled along, picking up speed now.

Cap bolted over to the window and pressed his face hard against the glass. I looked at his smudged, freckled face. What ever was wrong with him? He acted like he'd never been on a train before.

"Oh, no!" Cap moaned.

Winnie turned to me, her face white.

"What's the matter with you two?" I asked.

Winnie looked at Cap, then back at me.

"The train scene," she gasped.

"So?"

"So?" she screeched. *"So?* This is the movie's big finale! The train scene, you little idiot! The train—*this* train—plunges into the canyon and crashes to pieces on the rocks below."

A horrible chill swept through me. No! It couldn't be! But the look on their faces made me believe it. The train *was* going to crash!

I tried to stay calm, to think. We must get off the train—but how?

"I know," I said. "Let's just yell and wave and they'll stop the train."

Winnie shook her head. "No, no. There's no way to stop it."

"Why not?"

"No engineer!" she exclaimed. "He was supposed to jump off once he got it started. There's no one else aboard. Just us—plunging to our deaths!"

Cap piped up then. "That's it! We'll jump off too. C'mon."

He rushed back to the stuck door and yanked at the knob something fierce. The door still wouldn't budge. I joined him and together we worked at it. The doorknob rattled, then came off in his hand! I looked at the other door of the caboose, at the large padlock holding it shut tight. No way out there.

Could it really be we were stuck aboard a train hurtling to destruction? *No, Jessie,* I told myself. ***Think!***

I said, "They'll stop the train before it reaches the edge of the canyon. Surely they will."

Winnie shook her head. "Walt wanted the train wreck to look real," she said with a high, screechy voice. "He wanted it to be going really fast when it . . . when it crashed."

I stared blankly out the window. The barren Arizona landscape rushed by. An idea popped into my head.

"We'll break a window," I declared. "Then we can jump. There's no other way."

Winnie kept shaking her head, the craziness back in her voice. "I can't. I'll break my neck! It'll *ruin* me for the movies."

"You'll do a heap better in the movies alive than dead," Cap told her.

I glanced around, trying to spy something to break out a window. My eyes settled on the wooden crate.

I looked at Cap. He was staring at the crate himself. He glanced at me and nodded.

We ran over to the crate and dragged it to the stuck door. Then hoisting it up, we threw it at the window. The glass shattered. Jagged pieces stuck out around the edges like the teeth of some horrible creature.

Winnie cowered in the corner, her hands over her face. Cap picked up a chunk of the crate and hammered at the glass, trying to clear it all out.

"Come on, Winnie," I said. "You first. Climb out on the platform."

"No," she pouted, tears filling her eyes. "I can't do that. I can't jump."

"Why not?" Cap demanded.

"I don't do my own stunts! I'll get hurt!"

"You've *got* to this time," I pleaded. "Come on. You can do it. We'll help you."

Whimpering, Winnie let me lead her to the broken-out window. Cap got down on his hands and knees so she could step on his back and crawl through the opening.

After she plopped down on the platform outside, I called, "Just wait there, Winnie!"

Cap helped me up and out. Then I reached in to help him. I tugged hard on his arms. He managed to slither through. Finally, the three of us huddled on the platform together.

I took Winnie's hand, figuring she'd need some urging to jump. But at that moment she jerked her hand away, hopped down the two steps, put one hand on her head to hold her fake curls in place, and leaped from the train.

"Winnie!" I shouted. Cap and I leaned out, watching, as she hit the ground, tumbled a bit, and then picked herself up, her blond wig still atop her head. And all that from a girl who didn't do her own stunts! Winnie was full of surprises.

The train jerked on the track, throwing Cap and me back against the door of the caboose. Suddenly the door sprang open! We looked at each other. *The handcuffs,* I thought. *Just like those handcuffs last night.* If I hadn't had to face jumping off that train, I might've had a good laugh.

Cap leaned out, peering ahead.

"Look!" he yelled, pointing.

I looked. I spied people and cameras off to the left. That

must mean the end of the tracks, and the canyon, lay just ahead.

"Come on," I urged, tugging at his shirt. But inside I dreaded to jump. Doubts rose up to spook me. *Dear God, why? Why?*

The only answer came from Cap. "We've got to!" he shouted.

We scrambled to the bottom step and stood together a moment. Doubts kept flying through my mind. How could we jump? Even if we made it, we'd be hurt—and hurt bad. Abruptly, the train swung to the right. At that instant I got a glimpse of it.

The edge of the canyon!

This was it! At that instant I knew no matter how bad things looked, I had to rely on God. *Just let go, Jessie, and trust Him.* There was no other way.

We had to jump now or it would all be over.

Chapter 19

Time had run out. I prayed aloud as I bunched Cap's shirt in my fist, "Please, Lord, don't let us get hurt."

Then together we jumped.

"Aaaaaaaaahhhhhhhhh!" The breath seemed to suck right out of me as I hung in the air for an instant. Then I dropped, hard, to the ground.

I slid down a small slope and rolled a ways. When I stopped, I lay still on my back on the rocks, too stunned to move. Above, the clouds seemed to dance in circles in the brilliant blue sky.

Then came a tremendous roar.

CCCRRRAAAAAAAAASSHHH!

At first I didn't understand. Then it struck me. The train! I sat up suddenly, too suddenly. *Oh!* My head ached like the dickens and I felt dizzy. I grabbed my head, trying to steady the awful swirling. Slowly, I stretched out my arms and legs. My hand touched an object nearby. I heard a groan. Cap!

I turned toward him, squinting into the sun. He lay face down in the dirt. I forced myself to move and edged over to him. "Cap, are you all right?" I asked, laying my hand on his back.

He stirred, turned over slowly, and blinked at me. "Jessie?"

He knew me. A good sign, I thought, remembering what Tom had told me after I got blown up. I smiled at the boy.

"Thank goodness," he said. "I thought I was dead. And with the heat, I feared I might've gone to . . . "

A familiar voice broke in above us.

"I nearly broke my neck I'll have you know."

Winnie.

I turned around. She seemed just fine. The only harm I detected was the ripped skirt of her cowgirl outfit, a few dirty smudges on her face, and her fake blond curls turned around backward. She still held that silly fan.

Behind her I saw Tom rushing up. And behind him a whole slew of other folks.

"Jessie!" Tom cried, grabbing me and lifting me up. "Are you all right?" he asked, worry adding wrinkles to his face. As much as I ached, his hug felt good.

"Am I cursed or what?" Mr. Dixon's voice boomed behind Tom. "What do you little monsters think you were doing? You've just *ruined* my whole entire movie!"

I spied the red-faced director stomping around behind Tom. He'd already yanked off his safari hat and fired it to the ground.

Just then a thin man in a baggy undershirt and dark glasses raced up. "It's OK, Walt. We got it. We got the shot. The kids jumped before the train reached the cameras."

Mr. Dixon scooped up his ridiculous hat and planted it back on his bald head. "You got it?" he asked the cameraman like he didn't believe his ears.

"We got it," the man repeated.

"Good. That's good," Mr. Dixon said with a grin, the first I'd ever seen on him.

He took out his watch, consulted it, and snapped it shut. Then his eyes lit on Winnie. "Good gracious!" he exclaimed. "You all right, Winnie?"

"Just look at this *scrape!*" Winnie whined, pointing at her arm. I couldn't see a mark on it, but Mr. Dixon called for first aid.

"Why on earth were you children on that train?" Mr. Dixon asked, turning his attention to Cap and me.

Before we could answer, a man wearing a red baseball cap, Cap's father, broke through the crowd, swallowing his son up in his arms. Behind him rushed Iola and B.J.

Spotting them, Mr. Dixon said sternly to Iola, "I've been looking for you."

At first the vile woman stammered. She seemed plumb out of words. She pointed at me and cried, "That girl took my—"

"Took what, Iola?" Mr. Dixon interrupted. He reached into his pocket and pulled out a small black object. He flashed it in Iola's face. *The notebook!* "This?"

She didn't answer. He said, "I found this in my car. Tom tells me Jessie here came upon it." Then he demanded, "Explain it, Iola."

She glanced away, frowning, like she couldn't bear the

sight of the notebook—the evidence.

"Well, Iola, I'm waiting," he said. "And as you well know, I'm not a patient man."

Iola shrugged suddenly, as if unconcerned. "I don't know anything about that, Walt," she lied.

"These notations are in your handwriting. They seem to be a record of money. Money you've skimmed out of the movie accounts and into your own pocket!"

Iola shook her head. "I can explain, Walt," she countered, her voice trembling now.

"Explain this then," the director demanded, flipping through the notebook. "A little matter of four thousand dollars. Recorded right here." He jabbed his finger at the page. "Four thousand dollars the studio paid Flintrock for that train we just wrecked."

A gasp rose up from the townspeople surrounding us.

The director continued, "But really the town got nothing for the train, did it? It's *you,* Iola. You took the money for yourself. And that's only part of it."

Iola's eyes darted from side to side. She took a step back. She threw me an evil look, then pointed at B.J. "It's *him!* It was all *his* idea! He forced me to play along with him."

B.J.'s mouth dropped open. He scratched his head and knocked off his derby.

"Why, Iola, I can't . . . I just . . . " B.J. stuttered.

All around us the townspeople commenced to whispering. Not even Iola's own folks could believe for a moment her unlikely story.

Mr. Dixon slipped the notebook back in his pocket. "I'm turning this evidence over to the authorities," he said. "In fact, here's the gentleman we need right now."

A tall man with close-cropped brown hair emerged from the crowd. He wore a wrinkled, blue uniform with a silver badge pinned to his shirt.

"I'll attend to this," the police officer said. He took a pair of handcuffs from his belt and snapped them on Iola's and B.J.'s wrists. Real handcuffs. Then he led them away.

Iola's face had turned pure white. It matched exactly the color of the dead critter hanging around her neck.

Right then I almost felt sorry for her. *Almost.*

I did feel sorry for the poor B.J. Seeds, whose derby hat lay at my feet and who still trailed after Iola like a loyal puppy dog. He'd had the sad misfortune of turning his affection on the likes of her.

When they were gone, Mr. Dixon smiled at Cap and me and said, "One good thing. *Danger at Outlaw Creek* will have the best darn train wreck scene ever shot. It'll be marvelous. Audiences will just eat it up. It's just a darned lucky thing you kids jumped off before the train reached the cameras. For the sake of the movie, I mean."

I guessed I could be glad about that.

"Well, I'm certainly glad everything's rosy again," Winnie pouted. "Now, would somebody *please* attend to my injuries?"

Chapter 20

After that, it was a wrap, as Mr. Dixon said. The shooting of the moving picture ended that very day. Then the crew commenced taking apart the sets and packing up the equipment. I stopped by Winnie's trailer to say good-bye. Even though she acted like Miss Winnie Collins the famous child star again, I felt kind of sad. In a way, I'd miss the girl.

But I couldn't wait to go home. I'd had enough hair-raising adventures in Arizona. Besides, I missed Mama and Daddy something fierce. My almost-brother Leo Little Wolf would be arriving by train the next morning and then together with Tom we'd head on home. That evening I scrubbed off a few pounds of Arizona dirt and slept like a baby for the first time since I'd arrived.

* * *

The last morning I spent in Arizona Tom and I stood in front of the hotel talking with my new friend Cap McCall. The sun already blasted the street with a dry, furious heat.

I was all set to tell Tom and Cap about the lesson I'd

learned during my short stay in Flintrock. About how it didn't matter how many doubts leaped at me, I just needed to rely on the Lord. He'd never failed me. Not even once. And Flintrock had offered up plenty of doubts and dangers for the likes of me and Tom. But before I could get a word out, an excited and hatless Mr. Dixon ran up to us.

He gasped for breath, his bright red face now matching his sunburned, bald head.

"You'll never believe it!" he shouted. "It's *incredible!*"

"What on earth's happened?" Tom asked.

Mr. Dixon managed to calm himself a bit. "I've just come from seeing Winnie off. On the train to Los Angeles."

"Yep. And?"

"And I made the biggest discovery since—since Shirley Temple! Since Charlie Chaplin! Since *any*body! Audiences will fall in love . . . "

I heard someone stroll up behind Mr. Dixon. I peered around him.

Leo Little Wolf stood dressed in a fancy red cowboy shirt with pearl buttons. Mr. Dixon's too-big safari hat perched on his head, hiding his eyes. Leo's wild black hair poked out around his ears, and I saw his jaws working on a big wad of gum. Snuggled in one of his arms was my pet armadillo Victoria.

With his free hand my almost-brother began gracefully twirling a lasso over his head. Then he let loose and roped me! Yanking on the line, he pulled me close. Victoria leaned close and sniffed my face.

"Well, folks, I've done roped some mighty strange lookin' beasts before, but if this one don't beat all," he announced. "It's sure 'nough the strangest."

Very funny. I would've punched him if my arms hadn't been roped to my sides. Probably he knew that since he kept the rope cinched snug around me.

Mr. Dixon exclaimed, "Isn't he *great?* A natural! A boy Will Rogers! I can see it now. Dozens of movies—he'll be a *star!* Audiences will just eat him up!"

ABOUT THE AUTHOR

Jerry Jerman lives in Norman, Oklahoma with his wife Charlene, twin daughters Emily and Hadley, son Andrew, and two cats. He likes Mexican food, baseball, traveling throughout the American Southwest, and really fast roller coasters. When he's not writing about the journeys of Jessie Land, he keeps busy with church and family activities. Now and then he does something crazy like late October sailboat racing in a "frostbite regatta."

More Journeys of Jessie Land!

#1 The Long Way Home

When 12-year-old Jessie Land finds herself "dumped" on uncaring relatives, she determines to run away and find her parents in California. That means a desperate journey across the south-central U.S. during the Dust Bowl of 1935.

How will Jessie get from Liberal, Kansas to San Bernardino, California in only one week? That's all the time she has before her parents move on in their search for work.

Follow Jessie's exciting adventures as she joins two travelers, and stands up to danger and fear—armed with her faith, a tattered Bible, and her love for an orphaned armadillo named Victoria.

More Journeys of Jessie Land!

#2 My Father the Horse Thief

Jessie Land – happily reunited with her parents in California – soon finds herself in the middle of trouble.

Her father's new job on Will Rogers' Santa Monica ranch opens the door to disaster when Rogers' favorite horse, Soapsuds, turns up missing. Worse yet – Jessie's father also has disappeared. Soon after that, a ransom note for Soapsuds appears – in *his* handwriting.

With the help of her new friend, Leo Little Wolf, Jessie bravely searches for her father, encountering a dangerous wolf and even more dangerous men who want her father to be found guilty of the crime.

Join Jessie as she finds herself on a journey testing both her faith in God and in her father's innocence.

More Journeys of Jessie Land!

#3 Phantom of the Pueblo

What begins as an Arizona camping trip soon turns into trouble for Jessie Land and her almost-brother, Leo Little Wolf.

First, an old pueblo offers up a freshly hidden secret. Then Jessie and Leo confront one mystery after another. Who was playing that weird flute music in the pueblo? What creature left those odd tracks on the ground? What has become of their pilot friend Hazel Womack? And what about the mystery behind the phantom—whose presence seems all too real?

Added to this is the threatening figure of Cal Maddox, an unscrupulous rancher who threatens the pair at every turn. What is he after?

Join Jessie and Leo for their journey into danger, leading to discoveries of treasures of all kinds.